DORIAN ROCKWOOD

THE SILENT WITNESS MYSTERY

Also By Dorian Rockwood

Treachery Unmasked

The Cash Cache Mystery: a Case Twins Adventure

Chapter One

Dan Case squinted through the viewfinder of his camera, focusing on the cheerleaders clustering around somebody costumed as the high school's bear mascot. The sun bore down on them, casting long shadows across the glossy green football field. "Alright, girls, move in tight! You're looking great! Cozy up to the bear!" the seventeen-year-old called out, trying to hide his shyness behind an air of professionalism.

"Hey Dan, how many more pictures do you need?" The muffled voice of his brother Paul wheezed from beneath the bear's grinning face.

"Do not rush the official photographer of the 1948 Farmingford High School Bruin yearbook." Dan fiddled with his camera's exposure control.

The bear groaned. "I think I'm starting to cook in here."

"Where's your school spirit, my dear brother?" Dan held the camera up to his eye again.

"It melted."

"Quiet. Bears don't talk."

"This one does."

"Shut up." Dan made his last adjustments. "Almost done. We'll be finished after I grab a few more angles." He grinned and winked at the cheerleaders. "Maybe twelve or so more shots will do it."

"Oh, at least that many!" Donna flipped her auburn hair and smiled. "I want to make sure the camera gets my better side. Right, everyone? We need to look our best!"

All the cheerleaders agreed.

"I think it should be *two* dozen," Betty said. "I mean, if that is what our official photographer needs."

The bear growled and reached toward Dan with its paws.

"Perfect! That's perfect! Don't move!" Dan shouted. "Girls, move closer to the school mascot! I wish our football team was half as fierce!" Laughing, the girls grouped around the bear.

Dan kept calling out directions, asking one cheerleader to tilt her head one way, and another to face the camera a little more or move an arm slightly. He wanted to make sure the composition of the photo was exactly as he wanted it while he clicked off several additional shots. He finally lowered his camera with a satisfied smile. "Wonderful job, everybody. Thanks for your patience, especially to Mr. Bruin."

The bear took off his head, revealing Paul, Dan's identical twin. Both stood six feet tall, with brown hair and eyes. Paul's glasses and left-handedness were the way most people told them apart.

"Betty, help me out of this, will you please?" Paul thrust a finger at Dan. "Next time, my dear brother, I'm making you wear this rug while I take all the pretty pictures."

"Ha! You wouldn't know which end of the camera to look through. I'll keep taking the photos." Dan posed as if a statue and said in a lofty tone. "Besides, remember, sir, I am an artiste."

Paul rolled his eyes and groaned.

Betty passed her pom-poms to another girl and smiled at Paul. She took the head from him. "I kind of like you as a bear."

Dan put away his equipment and stood up. "You should meet him in the morning, then." Making a show of it, he bellowed, "I need coffee now!"

Betty chuckled as Paul stepped out of the mascot costume, dressed in jeans and by now a moist tee shirt. Handing the bear head to Donna, she gathered the rest of the costume. "Donna and I will come by tomorrow at five o'clock to pick you guys up. That'll give us time to eat before the movie. Sound like a plan?"

"Sounds like a plan." Paul gave Betty a quick kiss.

Donna performed a finger-twiddling wave to Dan. "See you then, handsome!"

Dan responded with a goofy, wide-eyed grin. Even after dating for a few months, he couldn't believe that the girl he considered the most beautiful in their small school liked him.

As the cheerleaders strolled away, chatting and laughing, Paul approached his brother. Dan picked up his camera bag and the two of them headed toward their army-surplus jeep parked next to the field.

Dan shot Paul a quick glance. "What's that smirk about?"

"You always blush when Donna calls you 'handsome'." Paul pinched one of Dan's cheeks and cooed. "It is soooo cute."

"Ah, get away with you." Dan swatted away his brother's hand. "You're jealous that Betty doesn't call you that. The nicest thing she ever says about you is 'Neanderthal'."

"That was so funny I forgot to laugh. Hardy har har."

"I'm surprised you understand what the word means," Dan said. "Are you still going to the YMCA?"

"Yeah. I need to practice walking upright without dragging my knuckles on the ground," Paul said dryly. "I'd also like to spar. At least get in a workout."

"What time should I tell Mom you'll be back?"

Paul checked his watch. "It's a quarter to four now, so around six... six-thirty."

"Try for six. I'm making chicken and rice for dinner tonight." Dan said as the two reached their jeep.

"I'll grab a burger on the way back." Paul took off the wet tee shirt and then rummaged through his gym bag.

"You don't know what you're missing, buddy."

"I do. That's why I'm grabbing a burger." Paul pulled another tee shirt out of the bag and slipped it on.

"Hey!" Dan protested. "Mom likes my chicken and rice!"

"She's being polite." Paul stuffed the dirty tee shirt into the gym bag and zipped it closed. "Hey, I hold up my end of our bargain to help her out now that she has been promoted to the lofty heights of management. How about that spaghetti I dished out on Tuesday night?"

"Came out of a can," Dan snorted.

"Yeah, but I opened it." Paul tapped himself on his chest.

"After I showed you how to use the opener."

"Funny guy." Paul gave Dan a light slap on the head.

"Do you want me to count to ten for you?" Dan said.

Paul looked puzzled. "Why should I want you to do that?"

"So you'll recognize it when you're sprawled flat on your back in the middle of the ring," Dan said with a sweet smile.

"Your faith in my skills is truly touching. How about a little demonstration?" Paul started throwing punches in his brother's direction.

Dan hopped backward, away from Paul. He began talking like a fight announcer as Paul pursued Dan, punching and jabbing. "And there's a left! And a right! And another left! Oh, Case is taking a terrible beating! It's amazing he's still on his feet!"

Paul slowly backed his twin against the open passenger side door.

"Ding! There's the bell ending the round, ladies and gentlemen! Back to your corner!" Dan scooped Paul's shirt off the seat and flung it at his twin.

Paul snatched the garment in midair and slipped it on, leaving it unbuttoned. He grinned. "You are so lucky the clock ran out, my dear brother." He climbed into the jeep and started the engine. "See ya later."

Dan gave a wave and began walking back to their home.

Paul shifted into first gear, pulled away, and turned onto Farmingford's main street, which did double duty as part of a state highway. He drove past the small town's businesses—the post office with its distinctive mailbox, the daycare center colorful with children's murals adorning the walls, and the library branch that waved the flag beside it. The church was a picture postcard sight as well, its white steeple standing tall against the pale-blue sky, nestled between what was rather grandly referred to as the "civic center" and an old oak tree. The town hall, a brick building, reached for the heavens with its tall pillars and a clock ticking every second.

The highway snaked its way out of Farmingford through the hillside woods, toward Belmont, the "big city" that had just passed its one-hundred-thousand population mark. The forests crowding the pavement were so dense with oaks and maples that they appeared almost impenetrable. As he drove on, there were small family farms spread between these trees; many of them tended by descendants of nineteenth-century settlers, tilling the soil for corn and hay while raising dairy cows, pigs, chickens, and sheep.

Not quite an hour later, he parked in front of the Belmont YMCA. Grabbing his gym bag, Paul jogged inside the building's locker room. He changed into his boxing shoes, trunks, and tee shirt, then slipped his glasses and watch into the locker and slammed the door shut. It reverberated against the white tile walls. After he grabbed his gloves and wrapping tape, he entered the gymnasium.

The pungent odor of sweat, combined with the distinct aroma of leather, filled his nostrils. The clang of metal coming from the small weight room echoed through the air, competing with the dull thuds of basketballs bouncing on the hardwood floor.

A corner of the large room was used by the boxing program. Only one other boxer, a tall teenager with a lean build and an unruly mass of blonde hair, stood by the ring, shadowboxing.

"Hiya, Paul!" Bud, who in his younger years had been a Golden Gloves champion and now coached boxers, gave Paul a hearty backslap as he came up. Paul returned the greeting. Bud cocked his head toward the other teen. "Fancy a few rounds with the new kid? I think he's got some skill."

Paul watched the other kid. It was clear he had been trained. "Yeah. I was hoping to spar some."

Bud said, "Sit tight. I'll check to see if he's interested."

Paul nodded in agreement and began some stretching. Bud went to speak with the boxer who had been sizing up Paul as well.

"Paul!" Bud waved him over.

"I'll be over!" Paul said. "Let me wrap up!"

He walked to the ring as he wrapped his hands. "Hey, I'm Paul."

"Jake," the other teen said.

"Nice to meet you." Paul gripped Jake's hand. He had a firm handshake. "Are you new around here? I don't remember seeing you before."

"Yeah, just moved here from Urbana." Jake's sharp features and his watchful yet wary eyes reminded Paul of a wolf.

"Belmont isn't the same as the big city!" Paul laughed. "Do you go to Belmont High?"

Jake shook his head. "McKinley."

"Glad to hear that! I go to Farmingford High, and Belmont is our arch-rival!" Jake didn't add anything or seem to care, so Paul tried to continue the conversation while he finished wrapping his hands. "What does your father do?"

"Ah, my old man walked out on Ma and me years ago," Jake said.

"Oh, sorry." Paul hurriedly put on his gloves, grateful for the distraction to hide his awkwardness. The twin's strong bond with their father sometimes made them forget everybody didn't have the same.

"That's okay," Jake dismissed. "The rummy wasn't much, even when he was sober."

"My Dad was killed in the war. On D-Day." Even though it was three years ago, Paul's voice caught in his throat.

"That's rough."

"Yeah, it is." Paul looked away as his eyes stung. He still missed his father.

"Let's start then, ready boys?" Bud helped Paul tie his gloves. "Three rounds. Keep it easy. I want to see how Jake handles himself."

Paul and Jake stepped into the boxing ring, ducking through the thick, coiled ropes. After they took their respective corners, Bud rang the bell.

The boxers approached each other and tapped their gloves. Paul began to circle his opponent, light on his feet and eyes constantly shifting. Jake stood tall with his arms raised in a defensive stance. Paul feinted for a jab, trying to catch Jake off guard. With lightning reflexes, Jake dodged the punch and countered with a strong right hook, colliding with Paul's jaw and seemingly ringing through the gym like thunder. Despite taking the hit, Paul remained composed and unfazed.

"Good shot," Paul complimented.

"Thanks," Jake said, maintaining his focus. "You're not too bad yourself."

"Pay attention to your footwork and maintain your balance, Jake!" Bud gripped the ropes and leaned on them. "Paul, keep a lookout out for those hooks. Pull your elbows in to protect your body!"

Paul unleashed a flurry of punches, each one with increasing force and determination. Jake ducked and weaved expertly, matching every blow with a punch of his own.

"Paul, breathe, relax, and conserve your energy between exchanges!" Bud coached. "Plan your strategy!"

Round after round they battled, neither fighter willing to give in. The sound of fists pounding on flesh and shuffling feet filled the ring, punctuated by strained grunts with powerful strikes. By the time the third round ended, their breathing had become ragged. Sweat glistened on their faces and soaked their tee-shirts.

"Alright, that's enough!" Bud rang the final bell. "Excellent workout, both of you."

"You've got some solid skills in there, man," Paul panted, touching gloves with Jake. "You took some heavy shots and kept going."

"Thanks. Your strategy was on the money... you caught me off guard a few times," Jake said.

"And you've got a strong gut punch." Paul patted his stomach.

Jake grinned. "It's my specialty."

Paul glanced at a small group of men and boys who gathered to watch the match. He chuckled as he nodded toward them. "The fans got a show tonight. I wonder if any of them placed bets."

Jake leaned into Paul. "Want to go another couple of rounds to give them their money's worth?"

Paul checked the wall clock, then shook his head. "Sorry, can't. Mom is going to expect me home soon."

"My Ma doesn't care when I get back," Jake boasted, although Paul thought he detected a note of sadness.

"Well, I'm going to catch a shower," Paul said. "Looking forward to our next session."

"Definitely!" Jake said. "Be seeing ya."

"See ya around. Night, Bud! Thanks!"

Paul left the ring, heading for the bench. He peeled off his sweat-soaked gloves. The sticky feeling of perspiration clung to his skin, and he couldn't wait to wash it away. He was already anticipating the relief of hot, steamy water.

When he reached the locker room, it was noisy with loud conversations and the sound of showers running. He stepped into a stall and gratefully let the steaming water flow over him, washing away all traces of fatigue. After drying himself off with a coarse towel, he changed into his clothes and went outside.

The early October night was still comfortably warm and balmy, with a slight chill hinting at the cooler months ahead. The luminous full moon shimmered brightly in the cloudless night sky, casting its dull silver light onto each car in the crowded parking lot, draining all the color from the world.

As he walked out of the building, Paul noticed two men leaning against the building in the shadows. They appeared to be in their forties and kept their eyes trained on him. The strangers were dressed head to toe in black suits and exuded an aura of dark foreboding, making Paul uneasy.

"Hey, kid," one of them said, pushing away from the wall and stepping into Paul's path, forcing him to stop. "We saw you fight in there. You handled yourself good."

"Uh, thanks," Paul answered cautiously, trying to gauge the intentions of the strangers. "Excuse me, do I know you?"

"I'm Ricco," the first man said, offering his hand for Paul to shake. "And this is my friend Vinnie."

Paul shook Ricco's hand briefly before turning to Vinnie and doing the same. His mind raced with possible reasons they wanted to see him, but each scenario seemed equally far-fetched.

"We want to talk with you a bit." Ricco jerked his head toward the parked cars. "You were heading for your car, weren't you? We'll walk along."

Paul hesitated for a moment, then nodded. He was ready to defend himself from the two men if he had to, feeling confident in his boxing skills. Still, there was a doubt lingering in his mind about whether he would be able to take them on both at once. The group started for the lot.

"Listen," Ricco scanned the area to make sure he wasn't overheard, his voice hushed and secretive, "like I said, we witnessed your power in the ring, and we believe—"

Paul interrupted him. "If you're managers or something, trying to sign guys up to box for you, I'm not—"

"Nah, nothing like that at all," Ricco said, a little too jovially. "We're not in the fight game. That's mostly crooked. We were wondering if you'd like to pick up some easy dough."

"Easy dough?"

"Yeah, yeah, you got it. That's the ticket. So simple you won't know you're doing it," Ricco said. "We thought you'd be perfect for a little... side job."

"Side job?" Paul's brow furrowed with confusion.

"Let me ask you something, pal. What do you do now for a little folding money? Anything?" Ricco asked.

"I do yardwork."

Vinnie dismissed Paul's answer with a contemptuous wave of his hand. "Bah, mowing lawns! What type of job is that for a guy who punches like you do? We're new in town, and we work for someone who could use a man like you, with your talent. You know, to help keep the customers in order. You know."

"No, I don't."

"Do I have to draw you a picture?" Ricco said in exasperation. "The boss would like somebody to help him out when he runs into trouble... you know, explain things to people. If they don't seem to be able to understand... or are behind on their payments. You know, be an enforcer."

"An enforcer," Paul echoed, his pulse quickening as the implications of their offer sank in. This was a gang, and they wanted him to join them.

"On the button," Ricco nodded, as though he read Paul's thoughts. "You'd be paid well, plus you'd have our protection. Think about it. Pays a lot better than pushing a mower."

Paul thought of the recent revelation about his father's past, how he had once been in a gang and how he got out; that made Paul admire his dad even more. He was determined to avoid his father's path of trouble, refusing to even start on that road.

"Thanks for the offer," he answered firmly and with a hint of sarcasm, trying to mask his unease with firmness, "but I'm not interested. You need to find yourself another boy."

"Really?" Vinnie raised an eyebrow in disbelief. "You sure about that? Easy money. Beats cutting grass."

"Positive," Paul met Vinnie's gaze without flinching. "I've got my own path to follow."

Ricco and Vinnie exchanged glances before shrugging nonchalantly. "Alright, kid," Ricco said. "We may drop around again. Just remember, the door's always open if you change your mind."

"I won't," Paul said.

The two men walked away, their black clothes melding into the night. Paul watched him until they disappeared into the darkness.

"Guess I'll just stick to boxing and mowing lawns," Paul muttered to himself. He headed toward the jeep. He felt he needed another shower to wash away the remnants of the encounter.

Chapter Two

Dan glanced at Paul, one eyebrow raised. "Ricco and Vinnie? You got to be kidding."

Paul lay stretched out on his brother's bed, fingers linked behind his head, already dressed for their date with Betty and Donna. He waited for Dan to change out of the outfit he wore for his job as a soda jerk at Allen's Drugstore. They both had worked all day, so they hadn't had a chance to talk with each other until now.

"Well, that's what they said, but they may not be their real handles." Paul gave a shrug.

"They sound like they came out of the 'Children's Garden of Gangster Names'," Dan untied and removed his bright red apron. Hanging it up, he took off his long-sleeved white shirt. He grabbed a hanger from the closet. "You said they offered you a job as a what? An enforcer?"

Paul nodded.

Dan aimed the hanger like a gun and imitated a movie hood. "Hey, bub, yous bedder pays up, or it's curtains for ya!" Hanging up the white shirt, he rummaged through his clothes, and took out a plaid one. He put it on while he shook his head. "Nah, you'd never amount to anything in that line of work. Your grammar is too correct."

Their mother's voice came from the living room. "Boys! Betty and Donna are pulling up!"

"Be right there, Mom!" Paul jumped off the bed and stopped Dan with a warning hand against his chest, wagging his index finger at his brother. "Don't tell the girls about this."

Dan spread his hands. "Why not?" He gave a growl, elbowed his twin in the side, and winked. "Come on, Betty may like it. Her boyfriend is a dangerous, rough, tough guy! Like from the pictures."

Paul grabbed his brother by the shirtfront and pulled him close. Playing the mobster role, he snarled, "Nah, you're wrong, pal, see? She likes me because I'm all gentle and sweet, see? I'm like a little furry kitten, see? A pussycat, see?"

"Boys! Don't keep your dates waiting!" their mother ordered.

"Coming!" The brothers responded as one and scurried out of the bedroom, Dan nabbing his camera as they left.

"Do you have to take that thing everywhere?" Paul said, as the two hurried down the hall.

"I want to ask Betty a favor." Dan slung the camera strap around his neck.

After a rushed "good night have fun thanks" exchange with their mother, the twins stepped outside. Paul slowed to an as-sured walk, which Dan copied, as they headed for Betty, sitting at the wheel of her family's convertible.

The girls didn't mind riding in the twin's jeep when they went swimming or playing miniature golf, but they drew the line when they all went out for "fancy dates": dinner and a movie. Then it was the droptop or nothing.

Dan climbed into the back with Donna, while Paul slid into the passenger side. As Betty drove toward Belmont, the group soon was talking, laughing, and singing along with the radio. Just as they reached the outskirts of the small city, Dan leaned over the front seat.

"When we reach town, Betty, could you turn on Brentwood, please?" Dan asked.

"Where the warehouses are?" Betty said over her shoulder.

"Yeah. I want to take a few shots for that streetscape painting I want to do," Dan explained. "Besides, I need to finish up this roll so I can develop it." He nodded toward his twin. "It's got some great shots of a grouchy bear on it."

Paul growled, "A detour for pictures? We're going to be late for the movie."

"Don't pay any attention to him. He gets upset if he misses the cartoon. Come on, Betty, it'll just take a minute," Dan urged.

Paul addressed the girls. "See? See the things I live with having an artist as a brother?" He pretended to be Dan. "Oh, look at that light! Oh, look at the colors! Wait, let me do a quick sketch!" Paul lifted his hands in resignation. "What's a guy going to do?"

"Quiet, or I'll hide your Roy Rogers coloring book," Dan retorted.

"All right, we'll go, we have the time," Betty laughed, "but you owe us all popcorn."

"The huge tub," Paul added.

"Soaking with what they pretend is butter," Donna put in.

"Deal, deal, and deal." Dan flopped into the back seat next to Donna.

Betty turned on Brentwood and parked the car on the street near an alley between two warehouses. The buildings were in a variety of shapes, sizes, and colors. They appeared stacked in every possible physical way, with alleyways barely wide enough for two cars to pass through.

The four climbed out of the convertible. Dan led the way through the crisp evening air to the alley entrance.

"Alright, this is perfect!" Dan said. "It's the golden hour! When the sun is down, but not yet set, you know. Wow, look—"

"At the light!" the other three chorused.

Dan turned to them and gave them a haughty glare. "Uncultured rabble," he sniffed. Raising his camera, he began to focus on the grimy brick walls and stacks of crates sitting on loading docks, bathed in the soft, warm light. "Oh, wow, this is perfect! It'll make a wonderful study." He clicked off a shot.

"Can we go now, Rembrandt?" Paul impatiently tapped his foot.

"Almost." Dan shifted right, looking for a better angle. At that moment, a faint sound of distress seemed to float through the air.

"Did you guys hear that?" Donna asked.

Betty nodded. "Sounded like someone yelling... maybe for help."

The group was completely alone in the street and the alley. They scanned their surroundings, searching for the source of the desperate call that they had heard.

The odd cry repeated, seemingly coming from directly underneath their feet.

Dan pulled his eye away from the viewfinder, but kept his camera held in his hands in front of him. "It must have come out of one of the buildings."

The foursome stood outside a building with the sign reading "Davis Farm Supply Company" painted on it, just a few paces away from an iron ventilating grating set in the pavement.

"Did it come out of that grill?" Paul pointed.

The heavy wooden door of the farm supply store creaked open, and a man wearing a black suit with his hat tugged down over his eyes hustled out. He tugged up his coat collar as he threw glances over his shoulder, a mysterious bundle pressed close against his chest. Turning to sprint down the alley, he noticed the group standing in front of him. Abruptly he stopped, hesitated briefly, then swiftly turned and fled.

"He's up to no good." Paul's voice was low and determined. "I'm going after that guy." Without waiting a moment longer, he took off in pursuit.

As Paul rushed around the corner of the warehouse, he locked onto his target's fleeing silhouette and his heart began to pound. With each step, his adrenaline surged, pushing him faster as he closed the gap between the two of them. He reached out his fingers, ready to grasp the man's collar, when something slammed into him from the side like a raging bull, knocking every ounce of air out of him.

Paul grunted as he impacted the wall. His assailant clung to his back like a leech, an arm locked around Paul's neck while his other arm was painfully bent behind him. Pounding footsteps approached from the alleyway and another pair of hands grasped at his legs, pinning him against the bricks.

Paul attempted to break free of the grip, but his opponents were too strong. With a quick heave, they tossed him in the air and pitched him into a dumpster. He landed face-first in the slippery slop of rotten vegetables, banana peels and yesterday's Blue Plate Specials that filled the bottom.

He swore loudly as he sloshed his way upright in the dumpster's load of broken eggshells, slimy lettuce, and sour milk. Pulling himself up, he hooked one leg over the metal rim and scrambled out of the smelly bin. The two figures he was chasing had already reached the end of the building, but he caught a glimpse of a tall, lanky figure with what seemed to be wild hair before they vanished around the corner.

Paul chased after them but then stopped when he heard a car speed away. He cursed as he brushed off bits of trash from his clothes.

***

"Paul, wait!" Too late. His twin was gone, swallowed up by the shadows. Dan grumbled with a wave of one hand, "There he goes again, charging like the Seventh Cavalry."

"Uh, guys..." Donna sniffed the air cautiously, "is it just me, or does anyone else smell something burning?"

They all fell silent, each one catching the faint whiff of smoke. Their eyes met, and at that moment, they knew something was definitely wrong.

The side door of the warehouse remained slightly ajar. Dan rushed over and pushed it farther open with the toe of his shoe. He glanced back at the girls and shrugged, then stepped inside the dark vestibule, followed by Betty and Donna.

"That's smoke all right, Donna!" Dan tried to keep his voice steady despite his nerves. "Call the police! Call the fire department! Call somebody! Call everybody!" He handed his camera to Donna. "I'm going to check if there's anybody down here."

"Dan, be careful!" Donna cried.

"Please, Dan!" Betty tugged on Donna's arm. "We'll be back as fast as we can!"

Donna and Betty ran outside, their feet pounding against the pavement. Dan clattered down a set of creaky wooden steps and into the dark basement, his fingers fumbling along the wall until they found a switch. A flood of blinding light filled the room, revealing dense black smoke billowing out from an adjoining doorway. The sound of crackling flames could faintly be heard from the next room.

He cupped his hands by the sides of his mouth. "Hello! Is anybody in here?"

A muffled answer came through the open door.

Dan spotted a fire hose nestled on a metal reel hanging on a wall. He rushed to it, pulled off a portion, and dropped it to the floor. Grunting, he turned the stiff valve to open it. No water.

In frustration, Dan kicked the useless hose away and dashed through the doorway. His heart pounded in his chest as he entered the room, only to be slammed with an overwhelming wave of intense heat. The acrid smell of burning wood filled his nose, causing him to catch his breath. Flames blazed against one wall, reaching up to the ceiling and sending thick clouds of smoke throughout the room. Instantly, sweat began to pour down Dan's face as the scorching heat seeped through his clothes. He quickly shielded himself with one hand and noticed something in front of him.

On the cement floor, writhing and twisting, lay a man, bound and gagged. Dan rushed over and dropped to his knees to free the man.

"Thank you," the man choked out once the gag was removed.

Dan tore at the ropes binding the man's wrists with renewed energy. "Are you all right?"

"Yeah, I think so."

Dan nodded as he finished untying the man and helped him to his feet.

The man gestured to a round rubber object, resembling a balloon, hanging on the ceiling from the ceiling. "That bladder is filled with gasoline. Once the flames reach it, they will make it explode, and the flames will spread everywhere."

Dan tried to grab the bladder, but the scorching heat drove him back. He pulled the man toward the doorway. "We should try to contain the fire in this room. At least keep it away from that gas."

"He shut off the fire sprinklers... the man who set this," the man said. "If we can get it back on, the water will soak this room. That'll slow it down."

"I'll get it. Where's the shutoff?"

The man pointed. "Outside the back door."

Dan turned and started up the steps. He was halfway up when he heard Paul's voice.

"Dan?"

"Down here, buddy!" Dan called back. "Turn on the sprinkler system valve! Out by the door!"

"Right!"

Dan sprinted back downstairs. The hose he had thrown down earlier twisted and whipped like an angry snake as water sputtered, then shot out of the nozzle. He grabbed it and fought against its pressure as he swept it into the next room, aiming towards the flickering flames. The man stood beside him, trying to fight back with an extinguisher. In a minute, Paul came to his brother's side, helping control the hose. The sprinklers came on, soaking the room with a deluge after a loud clank from the ceiling.

Sirens approached the building. The three kept a steady stream of water playing on the blaze, while the sprinkler system completed their work. The fire subsided, then went out in an angry hiss. Paul closed the valve feeding the hose.

"Guess we won't need the fire department after all," murmured Dan, gazing at the blackened wall. He put the hose down with a tired sigh. "Now let's get out of the firemen's way."

The group slowly went up to the alley. The man collapsed on a nearby crate. "You saved my life. How can I ever thank you?"

"You'll get our bill in the morning," Dan grinned. "What happened anyway? Who tied you up?"

"I'll tell you!" the man said. "My name is Sam Davis. This is my business. Last month, a man approached me, claiming to represent an insurance company."

"There's nothing wrong with that," remarked Paul.

"No, of course not, but it was the type of 'policy' he was offering that was. If I had paid over eight dollars a week, this person—he called himself Mac Slater—assured me my building would be safe from fire, damage, and other 'accidents'," Mr. Davis said.

"That seems expensive," said Paul.

"It is!" Mr. Davis nodded.

"You refused the offer, I'm guessing," Paul said.

"I did," Mr. Davis emphasized. "Then little things kept happening around the store... vandalism, broken windows, a trash can fire, things like that. Slater returned to sell me his 'insurance'. He implied he could stop those incidents, or make them worse."

"You mean it's some kind of racket?" asked Dan.

"That's the way I figured it," Mr. Davis said. "The insurance outfit is probably a dummy, set up for the sole purpose of forcing business owners to pay exorbitant sums for protection. Tonight proves I was right! I turned him down again, but I believed they would still try to get me. So I had the sprinkler system installed. Then I made a point of keeping constant watch of the building. Even slept here the past few nights."

"So, did you surprise someone firing the place?" Dan gestured toward the building. "That fellow we saw running away?"

"It was the other way around. He surprised me." Mr. Davis shook his head ruefully. "I was pretty tired, and nothing had happened for the past two weeks, so I dropped my guard. I seemed to have been sleeping like a log not to hear him enter the basement. He had set the fire when I woke up. I yelled for help, but he quickly overpowered me."

"Trussed you up and left you to burn?" Dan asked.

"Sure," said Mr. Davis. "He must have decided a dead witness is a silent witness. That way, I couldn't carry any tales to the authorities!"

"Did you get a look at him?" Paul asked.

Mr. Davis shook his head. "It was dark in there. But I know it wasn't the same man—that Slater guy—who originally tried to shake me down."

"You'll report all this to the cops, of course?" Dan glanced down the alley as a police car rolled up.

"Yeah, of course," the building's owner said with an apathetic shrug. "What help will that do? They've known about this criminal behavior for months now and, try as they might, they can't gather enough evidence to get them in court. The gang is cunning and may have influential connections who know how to keep them out of trouble."

The arrival of the fire truck cut the conversation short. Its piercing siren bounced off the walls of the buildings, filling the alley with a booming sound, while its revolving light cast an eerie red, pulsating hue over the scene. The firemen jumped out and began pulling hoses out of the back.

Betty and Donna rushed behind the truck, signaling the firefighters to the basement door. Their gazes landed on the boys.

"Dan! Paul!" they shouted with relief and rushed over to them. "You're safe!"

They threw their arms around the twin's necks, then immediately backed away.

"You're both soaking wet!" Betty waved her hand in front of her face and looked at Paul. "And you stink!"

"The guy I was chasing had a friend waiting in the back of the building." Paul looked down at the ground, embarrassed. "They... well... they pitched me into a dumpster."

"Oh, and here I thought it was another one of your new colognes." Dan continued in a French accent. "Arôme de garbáge."

Paul shot his brother the evil eye.

"I wouldn't talk, Dan." Donna drew a finger down his cheek. "It's like you've been shoveling coal! Covered in soot!"

"Don't be too hard on them, ladies. These two brave lads pulled me from the fire," Mr. Davis said.

"I always knew you were a hero, handsome," Donna smiled.

Dan hitched up his pants and spat. He tapped two fingers on his forehead and imitated a movie cowboy. "Ah, shucks, ma'am, it's just what us Case twins do."

Donna kissed Dan, then wiped her mouth with the back of her hand. "Ugh. You taste like an ashtray."

"Well, he looks like one," Paul fired in.

Dan mimicked the sentence back. "Brilliant retort, my dear brother. You must have exhausted all your brain cells on that one."

"Did that man we saw have something to do with the fire?" Betty asked.

"He started it," Mr. Davis answered.

"Unfortunately, I didn't get a chance to see his face when I chased him down the alley," Paul said, "other than he was about my height and wore a dark suit and a hat. Not a lot to go on. Any of you guys see anything more?"

Dan, Betty, and Donna looked at each other and shook their heads.

"He had his coat collar pulled up," Betty said. "I didn't see his face."

"Me neither," Dan shrugged.

"I was surprised by his sudden appearance," Donna shrugged. "I'm afraid I didn't pay attention."

"Paul, you told us somebody was waiting in the back alley," Dan said. "Did you get a clear view of that one?"

"No," Paul said. "He held me in a headlock, then the first guy returned and joined in, tossing me into the dumpster. By the time

I climbed out, they were disappearing around the corner. I only caught a glimpse. They may have looked familiar, but…" Paul thought for a second, then shrugged. "I can't be certain."

"Well, there is one thing for sure," Dan said. "We all just came face-to-face with an arsonist."

Chapter Three

The group was quiet for a moment, and then Donna spoke to Mr. Davis. "I'm sorry we couldn't get a better description of him."

"You saved my life and my building! That's more than enough!" Mr. Davis said. "It was lucky you kids were here tonight. How come?"

"My brother has delusions he's an artist—" Paul started.

"Like he believes he's the next Joe Lewis," Dan tilted his head toward his brother.

"Pay no attention to him," Donna waved Paul off. "Dan's actually quite talented."

Dan smiled thanks to Donna. "I came here to take photos for a painting. I'm planning to do a streetscape."

"He's branching out from matching paint to the little numbers on a picture," Paul said.

"He's jealous I can count," Dan jerked his thumb at Paul.

Donna turned to Mr. Davis. "They act like that all the time."

"Just ignore them," Betty said.

"That's what we do. Here's your camera, handsome. All in one piece." Donna handed it to Dan with a smile.

"Thanks." Dan grinned back, his cheeks turning hot. Paul snickered. Dan nailed him with a poisonous look.

"I'm surprised he's not taking pictures now for a work entitled," Paul spread his hands wide, as though displaying the words in the air, "'Fire Engine in Alley'."

Dan snapped his fingers. "That's the best idea you've had for a while, my dear brother."

"Oh, no," Paul looked at the girls and groaned. "What have I done now?"

"Not pictures for a painting, stupid, but for the newspaper. Latest news, and all that. I might be able to sell a couple of photos to them." Dan turned to Mr. Davis. "Do you mind if I grab one or two?"

"Go ahead. Take as many pictures as you like. It's the least I can do," Mr. Davis said.

"You'll have to hurry." Betty indicated the approaching policeman with a nod of her head. "We're going to have a visitor soon."

"We'll give our statements first, to let you have more time to shoot," Paul said to Dan as he shooed him away. "Go! Quick! Make with those pretty pictures!"

"Thanks, buddy! Come on, Mr. Davis." Dan and Mr. Davis jogged back to the basement.

Downstairs, Dan captured two photos of Mr. Davis: one with the ropes that had bound him, and another set against the backdrop of the smoldering rubble. Then he shot a third picture of one of the firefighters inspecting the rubber bladder that held the gasoline and more of the overall damage.

A policeman met Dan and Mr. Davis when they came out of the building. "Can I please have a word with you both? Mr. Case, let's start with you. Step over here, sir. Can you tell me what happened?"

Dan described in detail the events that had taken place, answering the policeman's questions. After he was finished, the officer gave a small nod to the camera. "Is there anything inside that could help us?"

"I'm sorry, I'm afraid not. Donna, my girlfriend," Dan pointed her out, "was holding on to it during the excitement. She and Betty went to call the fire department."

"Too bad," the policeman said. He confirmed Dan's contact information. "You and your friends are free to go. In case any additional information is needed, a detective will call." The officer turned to Mr. Davis. "And you, sir?"

With a wave to Mr. Davis, Dan walked back to Paul, Betty, and Donna. "I guess we can scram."

The four returned to the convertible in silence. Just as Paul reached for the car door, Betty stopped him.

"My dad would kill me if I got the upholstery dirty, even for two heroes. There are blankets in the trunk. You and Dan wrap yourself in them," she said.

"And sit in the back," Donna pointed at Paul. "Especially you, stinky."

The brothers did impressions of children caught making a mess. "Yes, ma'am," they chimed together. Getting the blankets out and throwing them over the back seat, Dan and Paul climbed in.

"I don't think the theater will let those two in." Betty slid behind the wheel. "We'll head back to Farmingford and stop by the drive-in for burgers,"

"Let's get the food and bring it out. We'll eat in the car. Outside. In the fresh air," Donna threw a glance at the boys. "Betty, park in the far corner of the lot. These two could be mistaken for hobos."

"Sorry about missing the show, girls," Dan said. "With my detour and all."

Donna turned back from the front seat. "Who cares about the movies? Handsome, we were part of one!"

***

The next morning, Mrs. Case put down her coffee mug with a thunk. "You didn't see the picture last night because of what?"

The family sat in the kitchen breakfast nook, with the sun shining through the window. The siblings occupied one bench while their mother was on the one opposite. Mrs. Case was an attractive woman in her mid-thirties, equipped with an unexpected toughness that served her perfectly when she had to go toe-to-toe with city council members or meter readers as the first woman county water department manager.

Dan buttered a slice of toast and answered in a nonchalant tone. "No movie for us, because we saved a man from a burning building."

Paul nudged his brother. "If you want to be accurate, only a single room was on fire."

"It would have been the whole place if the sprinklers didn't come on," Dan said as he took a bite of his toast.

"Which I turned on." Paul pointed his fork at himself.

"After I told you where the valve was," Dan reminded him.

Their mother sounded a warning with an irritated breath.

"Okay, okay. Here's the true and actual story of how Dan and Paul Case saved a man from a fire." Dan leaned toward Mrs. Case to begin.

"It really should be how Paul and Dan Case rescued a man from a raging inferno," his brother said. Dan gave him a kick in the ankle under the table. "Ow."

"Boys!" Mrs. Case commanded.

The twins grinned as they eagerly jumped into their tale, bouncing off each other's words and interrupting to add a detail here or there. Their mother listened intently, her lips pursed into a thin line, her eyebrows raised, as though not wanting to believe what her sons told her, but knowing full well it was the truth. The story ended, and she stared at them for a long moment before speaking.

"Of course, I'm proud of the actions of you both." She gave them a warm smile, then she shook her head. "It's a mystery how you two are always in the right place when trouble begins."

"It must be our tarmac," said Paul.

"Karma," Dan and Mrs. Case automatically corrected.

"That too." Paul popped some toast into his mouth. He chewed for a second. "I don't get why an insurance company would burn down a building it wanted to insure. I mean, they would lose money. It doesn't make sense."

"It's a protection racket," the twin's mother said in a matter-of-fact tone, as though saying her coffee mug was green. "Rizzo had his hand in some. They're a nasty business."

Dan and Paul shared a knowing look. They'd recently found out when their parents were teens during Prohibition, they had been part of Lorenzo Rizzo's bootlegging gang in Chicago, although Mrs. Case assured them they weren't involved in any of the "rough stuff". Rizzo got gunned down by rival mobsters, their father barely escaping with his life. After that, their parents fled the city, settled in Farmingford, and made a new life for themselves.

"Protection rackets are all about fear and intimidation," Mrs. Case said. "They prey on innocent people, forcing them to pay 'tribute', it's called, for 'protection' they don't need. If they refuse, let's say accidents start to happen. Bigger and bigger ones until they start paying."

"Like what?" Dan's curiosity was piqued.

"Arson, vandalism, assault... you name it," came the grim reply.

"Why don't the victims call the cops?" Dan asked.

"Because getting the police involved would guarantee something bad would happen," Mrs. Case said. "Perhaps something fatal."

"But why in Belmont?" Paul shrugged. "It's not that big. I mean, there can't be as many targets as Chicago or New York. It would be harder to keep quiet in a smaller place, too."

"Maybe the gang is expanding, or testing the waters." Dan thought for a second. "They might be on the move, planning to shake down Belmont businesses briefly before moving elsewhere."

"All those are possible," Mrs. Case stated. "Finish up. It's time to get ready for church."

The boys changed clothes after services and went outside. Paul pulled a small notebook from his hip pocket and flipped through the pages.

"I only have the Mitchels and Jensens scheduled today." He slipped the pad away. "They're easy—just mow and rake jobs. You don't work tonight, do you?" Dan shook his head. "Is it okay to use the jeep?"

"Sure," Dan said. "I'm going to develop those pictures I took last night. I'll take them to the *Weekly* tomorrow after school, and see if I can sell them."

Paul clamped Dan on his back and announced. "Ladies and gentlemen, I give you my brother, Flash Case, Crime Photographer!"

"You'll be sorry when I win my Pulitzer!" Dan waggled his finger at Paul.

"That'll be quite a while."

"Not as long as yours to become the World Heavyweight Champion."

Paul stepped back, pretended to push up the sleeves of his shirt, and moved into an exaggerated boxer's pose. "Why, I oughta—"

Dan put one hand to his ear. "Hark! Do I not hear the Mitchels' lawn mower calling your name? Not to mention the song of something folding and green that isn't grass?"

"Okay, okay! I'm going!" Paul hopped into the jeep.

Grinning, Dan headed to the workshop he and Paul shared, built along one side of their home's detached garage. The room was narrow, and divided in half: one part held Paul's boxing gear—a beat-up punching bag, dumbbells, jump ropes, and gloves—and the other served as Dan's studio. A creaky oak stool stood in front of his easel by the window, worn where he always sat. Years of spilled paint discolored the table by the door. On top of it, his stacks of sketchbooks were organized with the most recent on top and older ones beneath them.

Dan stepped through the connecting door into the dim garage and headed for a makeshift darkroom the brothers had built in one corner. It was cramped, like a small closet, with only enough space for one person to stand. A counter was fixed to the wall, with two trays lying on it. Shelves below held containers of various chemicals used to develop film. Dan pulled the heavy blackout curtain closed behind him and began to work.

The sharp stink of the developers filled the small space, but Dan didn't notice as he gazed at the tray in front of him. He always enjoyed watching the photographs develop, as small black dots slowly appeared and formed an image on the white paper. His smile widened as a picture took shape of Paul in the bear costume surrounded by the gleeful cheerleaders. He knew one of these shots would make it into the yearbook. Hanging the photos up to dry, he moved on to the ones he had taken at the fire.

Holding a magnifying glass, he scanned each picture for any clue that could lead closer to finding the arsonist or ending the protection racket. Although nothing caught his eye, he was quite satisfied with the quality of his photography as added the prints to the drying line. He grinned.

"Mighty fine job, Flash. Mighty fine," he said to himself.

***

The two brothers headed to Belmont Monday after school. Paul used Dan's errand as a chance to go to the YMCA. After dropping Paul off, Dan drove to the local newspaper, the *Belmont Weekly*.

Dan entered the office with what he hoped was a determined stride, passing walls adorned with framed front pages of the newspaper, screaming headlines of past events. The air was thick with the smell of ink and newsprint. Typewriters clattered in nearby offices and ringing phones filled the building with a sense of energy. He tucked the envelope of his prints under his arm and approached Mr. Thompson's desk where he sat, squinting through wire-rimmed glasses at a stack of papers.

"Excuse me, Mr. Thompson?" Dan tried to get the editor's attention.

"What do you want, kid?" Mr. Thompson barked, not bothering to look up.

"Um, I have some photos I took a couple of nights ago," Dan attempted to sound confident, despite holding the envelope out in his shaking hand. "I think they might be of interest to your newspaper."

"Don't need any pictures of the high school football game, kid," Thompson scowled. "Or cute babies, or cute kittens or cute puppies, or cute anything."

"These are of the Davis warehouse fire," Dan said. "I was there."

"What, huh?" Mr. Thompson finally looked up from his work and gave Dan his full attention. "Alright, show me what you got."

Dan took a deep breath and spread out the glossy photographs on Mr. Thompson's cluttered desk. The editor studied each image. He seemed to linger a bit longer on the shots Dan took inside the warehouse.

"Not half bad, kid," Mr. Thompson said grudgingly, tapping the prints. "You said you were on the scene?"

"Yes. My brother and I helped put the flames out. We were there before the fire department."

"Rewrite!" Mr. Thompson yelled, not taking his eyes off Dan. "As a rule, we don't pay for freelance work, especially from amateurs." He crossed his arms over his chest and leaned back in his chair, considering Dan. Out of nowhere, a tall, skinny man appeared next to the desk. "Alright, I'll give you ten bucks each for the usable ones, plus you tell your story to Hank here."

"Make it twenty-five and you've got a deal," Dan countered, surprising himself with his boldness.

"Twenty-five? Of all the highway robbery..." the editor sputtered. Despite his grumbling, a small smile played at the corners
of Mr. Thompson's mouth. "Kid, you've got some nerve. I
admire that. Okay, twenty-five it is." He pointed to emphasize
what he said next. "Don't expect this to become a regular thing."

"No, sir, I won't. Thank you, sir," Dan said with a smile.

Mr. Thompson gathered the photos and handed them to the
man. "Hank, we'll run his story as a sidebar. Kid, tell what
happened to Hank." Mr. Thompson returned to the copy on
his desk as Dan followed Hank to a different part of the office.

***

Once he had changed his clothes, Paul stepped into the YMCA's
gym, looking around the boxing area for a familiar face. His eyes
rested on someone with a slim build and blonde hair. It was
Jake, working on one of the speed bags. Paul briefly thought he
looked like one of the people from the fire the other night.

He couldn't be sure, given how little he saw of the others
as they turned the corner. Many Swedish people settled in the
area during the 1800s. Plenty of blonde hair to go around. Even
though the two only just met before beginning their sparring
session, Paul liked Jake and hoped he wasn't involved in a protection racket.

Still, Paul was unsure about the other boy, and he wanted to
figure out the source of his unease. Walking up and asking him if he
helped an arsonist last night was out. He wished Dan was here; he

knew how to question better than Paul. Despite this, Paul decided to explore on his own.

"Hey, Jake," Paul strolled over. "Up for a few rounds?"

"Sure thing, Paul." A smirk played on Jake's lips. "I'm always up for putting you in your place. Flat on the canvas."

"Keep dreaming that dream, buddy," Paul said. He started to wrap his hands. "What about what happened downtown last night?"

Jake hesitated a second before he answered. "You mean something finally happened in this burg?"

"Yeah. I was wondering if you knew anything more about the excitement." Paul kept one eye on Jake while he finished wrapping. "You know about the big blaze, don't you?"

"Nah, I don't pay attention to the news." Jake crossed his arms.

"Well, it happened down on Brentwood, where all the warehouses are. I heard the fire was at the building for Davis Farm Supply." Paul put on his gloves, trying to see if Jake had any reaction to what he said. Jake's face was impassive, other than a slight twitch of the lower lip.

Jake shrugged, pulling on his gloves. "I don't even know where that street is. I'm new around here, remember?"

"Oh, yeah. I forgot." Paul continued as they stepped into the ring. "It seems like two people set the fire. I heard some guy chased one of them down an alley. Almost caught him too."

Jake's eyes narrowed, as though trying to place Paul. "Sounds like a real hero." Something in his tone betrayed nervousness.

"I don't know if I could do something like that," Paul pressed, hoping to catch Jake off guard. "I mean, chase somebody. A criminal."

"Me neither. I ain't no lawman," Jake scoffed.

Paul figured he was getting nowhere fast. "Alright, let's get started."

He hammered the button on the timer and met Jake in the center of the ring. Paul raised his gloves. Jake mirrored the action, his eyes locked on Paul's. The two touched gloves.

"You handled yourself well the last time. Let's see what you bring now, pretty boy," Jake launched a lightning-fast jab that Paul narrowly dodged.

"Nice try," Paul retorted, throwing a punch of his own.

The sparring match continued. Paul and Jake circled each other, each fighter's eyes trained intently on their opponent. Paul jabbed forward, but Jake was quick to dodge and counter. He rained down punches from all angles as Paul blocked and weaved. Both glistened with sweat, Paul's brown curls clinging to his forehead, and Jake's golden hair matted down. The timer rang out, signaling the end of an intense round with no clear winner. They touched gloves again.

"Good workout," Paul panted.

"Yeah." Jake wiped the perspiration from his forehead with one forearm. "One day, one of us is going to be standing and one's going to be on the mat."

Paul looked out at the gym. "We don't have as many spectators as we did the last time we sparred."

"There's probably something good on the radio," Jake laughed.

"Maybe. You know, I don't see those two guys," Paul said.

"What two guys?" Jake's voice was tinged with suspicion.

Paul faced his opponent. He made one final attempt to rattle Jake. "They were big, tough looking. Wore black suits. Hung out in the back."

That had an effect. Jake seemed to flinch in recognition, his face blanching beneath a thin sheen of sweat. "I don't remember them."

"They reminded me of gangsters." Dan laughed, then stepped closer. "I have a relative—a very close one—that was once part of a Chicago gang during Prohibition. He almost lost his life because of it."

"Interesting story. So why are you telling me?" Jake walked toward the ropes. "I gotta get home. My ma is expecting me."

"I thought you said your mother didn't care when you got in," Paul said.

Jake shot Paul a poisonous look as yanked off his boxing gloves. He left the ring without another word and strode out of the gym.

Paul couldn't shake the feeling that the descriptions of Ricco and Vinnie struck a nerve. He replayed their conversation in his head, searching for any other clues that might confirm his suspicion. But no matter how many times he went over it, one thing remained clear: if Jake was involved, he wasn't going to give himself away that easily.

Chapter Four

Paul dragged himself home at five o'clock in the afternoon, exhausted from toiling away in Mrs. Carmichael's garden. Every time he worked there, he wondered if it was worth having to labor under her ever-present and exacting supervision. However, she paid the most of all his clients and tipped him generously, so greed won in the end. While there, all he could do was surrender and give his best effort. He gave with a long sigh and stretched. But boy, did working at her house tire him out.

His mom was attending a city council meeting, and Dan was at his job. With the house to himself, he could listen to whatever radio program he wanted without putting it up for a vote. Stripping off his sweaty tee shirt, he made a beeline for the bathroom. He couldn't wait to wash away the perspiration and grime that clung to him like a second skin.

He looked forward to a soak in a hot bath as he entered the small tiled room. Peeling off the rest of his clothes, he stuffed them haphazardly into the dirty laundry hamper. Wrapping a towel around his waist, he bent down and start filling the tub with water, adjusting the knobs until steam rose. The sound of the filling tub, rhythmic and soothing, let him forget momentarily his tired muscles. He took off his glasses and put them on the sink.

He stood there, lost in thought, when a sudden noise from the kitchen startled him back to reality. Paul furrowed his brow, wondering if his mother had already returned from the city council meeting.

"Mom? Is that you?" Paul's voice echoed down the empty hall. "Did you get lucky, and the meeting ended early? I know how much you hate them."

A brief pause came, then unmistakable shuffling footsteps and the back screen door closing. Maybe Dan returned from the drugstore and was sneaking up on him as a prank.

"Dan, if that's you, better answer me right now." Paul's tone was laced with both irritation and frustration. "I'm not in the mood for a prank. I worked hard today. You're not being funny. Knock it off."

Paul held his breath and waited, listening intently for the slightest noise. All he heard was the clock ticking in the hallway. He inched towards the door, pressing his ear against it in hopes of hearing something. For a moment, he thought he heard some faint rustling noises, but soon the silence returned.

Before Paul could decide his next move, the bathroom door burst wide open and two strangers forced their way in. The men wore bandannas, hiding their faces except for their glinting eyes that were shadowed under pulled low hats. They pushed Paul until he backed into the towel bar.

"Listen punk, give us the negatives of those pictures and everything will be okay," one man said in a harsh whisper, his voice muffled by the fabric.

Paul's emotions warred within him; anger and fear boiling over as he stared at the intruders. Anger won. "Why should I let you have them? Who do you think you are, barging in like this?"

The first man stepped closer, eyes narrowing to menacing slits. He thrust his one finger into Paul's face. "Do it now, if you know what's good for you."

Paul snarled as his boxing instincts kicked in and he threw a right hook at the man. His reflexes were no match for the tight quarters of the room. His foot slipped, sending him flying past his target and crashing onto the tile floor.

The second man grabbed Paul's arm, wrenching it up behind his back with enough force to make the joints creak. His teeth gritted together in agony as a cry of pain escaped his lips.

"Are you going to get us those negatives?" the first man growled. "I'm losing my patience."

Paul understood his only escape was to delay until another person arrived, potentially scaring away the men. "I don't know what you're talking about!" he shouted, his voice quivering from the pressure on his arm. "My brother is always taking pictures, but I don't know where he keeps his photography stuff! Let me go, and I promise to try my best to find them. But right now... with my arm twisted like this... I have no way of doing anything."

The second man snarled, tugging at Paul and yanking him more upright.

The first man planted his fists on his hips, and his voice was cold and unforgiving. "I don't believe you. We think you know exactly where they are. Yeah, you know, we are sure of it. You've wasted enough of our precious time already." He casually waved toward the other man. "Help him with his memory."

The man's grip tightened like a vise around Paul's arms, and with brute strength, he forced him down to his knees at the edge of the bathtub. "You think this'll give you a thought?" the second man growled. He shoved Paul's head under the water.

***

Dan scrubbed the marble soda fountain, then he buffed it dry. When he finished, his eyes settled on the small glass jar that held his tips. He gave it a shake and smiled. It had been a good night. He emptied the coins on the counter and counted out a few.

"Madge, hold on!" He waved at the gray-haired cashier by the drugstore's front door. "Don't close out yet! I want to make a purchase!" He pulled a few copies of the *Belmont Weekly* off the newsstand and rushed to the cash register. "Here, I'd like these."

Madge looked up from the drawer with her half-glasses perched on her nose. She adjusted them as she squinted at Dan. "Three copies of the *Weekly*?" she asked Dan. Her wrinkled hands moved with practiced ease as she punched the buttons of the cash register, each thump followed by a ringing chime.

"Yeah. One for me, one for Paul, and one for Mom." Dan held up the first page with pride. "See, they used one of my photos of the fire, right on the front page!" He pointed to a line of type. "I even got a credit. Look here! 'Photo by Dan Chase.' Oh, and check this article: 'Teens Rescue Man from Blazing Warehouse: Their Story.' That's Paul and I."

Madge's mouth turned up in a smile. "Are you certain you only want three copies?"

Dan grinned and gave a shrug. "Sure. I mean, I should leave a couple of others so more people can read of the Case twin's brave exploits." The two laughed as Dan dropped the coins into Madge's open hand. "Thanks. 'Night, Madge."

"Good night, hero," Madge said.

Dan stepped out the front door and took a deep breath. He pulled off the clip-on bow tie and opened the top buttons on his shirt. He looked at the newspaper again. "Dan Chase, Crime Photographer!" He chuckled aloud. "Well, if I can't make my art pay, there's always the news biz."

Paul needed the jeep for his afternoon landscaping job, so Dan tucked the papers under one arm and set off on the short walk home. It was a beautiful autumn evening, the sky an endless canvas of navy blue, pricked with stars just beginning to shine. The fresh air was brisk, and the auburn, burgundy, and vermilion leaves crunched beneath his feet.

Fifteen minutes later, he reached his house. The jeep stood in the driveway, but his mom's car wasn't there. The city council meeting must be going overtime, as usual. He noticed the house was dark.

"Paul? Are you here?" Dan called as he let himself in the front door, tossing the papers on the sofa. "Paul?" He went up the hall and poked his head inside his brother's room. It was empty.

Puzzled, Dan stepped across the hallway and knocked on the bathroom door. He got no response, so he pushed it open and flipped the switch. The sight of the bathtub, water sloshing over its side, sent a chill through him. Puddles formed a trail, pointing down the hallway. A feeling of panic clutched Dan's chest.

"Paul? All you all right? Answer me!" Dan's voice cracked with worry as he tracked the water to the back door. He went out onto the back porch and called. "Paul!"

Some bumps came from their workshop. Jogging across the yard, he opened the door. Paul was on the floor, gagged with a painting rag and hogtied by one of his jump ropes. Dan dropped to his knees next to his brother and removed the gag. "Are you okay, buddy?"

"Yeah. Just get me loose," Paul grumbled as Dan quickly untied him.

"How did this happen?" Dan helped his twin to his feet.

"I was jumping rope too fast, and I got tangled up. What do you think?" Paul shot back.

"Down, Spot, down."

Paul rubbed his wrists. "Some guys broke in. They thought I was you."

"Well, who were they?" Dan asked. "What did they look like?"

"It was two men. They wore bandannas over their faces, hats pulled down... they talked in a whisper, maybe to disguise their voices. I think there was a third person in the house, but I'm not sure." Paul snatched up the jump rope and hung it on its hook. "They forced me to take them to your negatives."

"Why did they want them? What for?" Dan tossed the rag on the table.

Paul shrugged. "One way to find out."

"Well, come on, let's check." Dan led the way to the darkroom. As they entered, Paul flicked on the red-tinted light, casting an eerie glow over the space. Dan flipped through a box filled with envelopes containing his negatives, and it didn't take long for him to find out which one was missing.

"That's it," Dan said as he tapped the container. "They took the negatives from the last roll of film I developed. It included the ones I took at the warehouse fire. They must have been after those."

The two went back into the workshop. Paul leaned against a wall. "We need to figure out who these guys are, my dear brother. They knew about your photos. Their visit must be connected with them somehow."

"Right," Dan nodded, his mind racing with possibilities. He sat on the stool. "Which means they have to be involved in the protection racket. It's the only logical answer for who would be interested in the pictures. But what's the reason?"

"What if they're trying to cover their tracks? It could be they thought you caught a picture of some kind of clue... something the cops would find useful," Paul suggested.

"That could be," Dan mused, his brow furrowed in concentration. "That guy—the arsonist—charged out of the warehouse basement and almost ran into us. He must have noticed I held a camera. I didn't get any pictures of him—I'm sure of that—but those goons don't know I didn't take one. Maybe they're scared. They thought I took an incriminating photo and want to get their hands on it."

"Exactly," Paul nodded. "If they believed we had evidence, they'd do anything to get it, like breaking in and dunking heads. But wait, why now? The fire was days ago. Why come after the pictures now?"

"Perhaps they weren't sure they existed before," Dan said. "They're still running around, so the cops haven't picked them up. That may have led them to think they were in the clear. Then the current issue of the *Weekly* hit the stands today with a front-page story about the fire, using one of my photos."

"Okay, but how did they find out you took it? You didn't give a business card to the guy in the alley."

"The paper gave me a credit line," Dan explained. "We're also in a side story about how we saved Mr. Davis. Bingo! There are our names in black and white: Dan and Paul Case of Farmingford. They only needed to find us in the phone book. We're the only Case family in town."

"Maybe we need to get an unlisted number," Paul muttered.

"Hey, Paul," Dan leaned forward on the stool. "Do you think you could recognize these guys if you saw them again? Or describe them to the cops?"

Paul shook his head and blew out his breath in frustration. "Nothing that would stand up in a court of law. Their faces were covered and with those hats pulled down... I'm not sure. But... but I certainly got a funny feeling..."

"About what?"

"I have a feeling they could be the same pair who talked with me at the YMCA."

"Really? Mutt and Jeff?" Dan's eyes widened in surprise.

"Ricco and Vinnie," Paul corrected.

"Yeah, those two," Dan said. "Didn't you tell me you thought there were over two of them tonight? Who's mysterious visitor number three?"

"I don't know." Paul gave a shrug. "I thought I heard someone else in the house, then they left. Whoever it was didn't join the party in the bathroom, but they were in the kitchen."

"Wow," Dan said. "It's getting more complicated every minute. We may need a program to tell the players."

"You said it." Paul's gaze drifted to the window as if expecting the intruders to reappear in the backyard at any moment. "What do you think our next move should be? I mean, do we tell Mom about what happened?"

Dan hopped off the stool and paced. "I don't know. I don't want to lie to her."

"Neither do I," Paul said, "but knowing that some thugs broke into our house and attacked me... she'd be beside herself with worry."

"I don't want to do that to her, either," Dan said, biting his lip as he considered their options. "Of course, if she doesn't know what went on here tonight, she wouldn't have to ask about it, then we wouldn't have to answer, so we wouldn't need to… well, let's say 'not tell the truth'. Technically speaking."

Paul shook his head. "I don't know… I don't like that. It sounds, well, borderline dishonest."

"That's because it is," Dan admitted. "Look, you weren't hurt—"

"True, only a little waterlogged. They took nothing valuable, only your pictures—"

"Well, thank you!" Dan huffed.

"Oh, you know what I mean…"

Dan thought for a second. "Okay, how about this? We'll come clean with her after this mess is cleared up, or at least when we're sure those guys won't pay a return visit. Let's keep this between us until then. Agreed?"

"Agreed," Paul said. "I think we should talk to the detective in Belmont handling the case. The information we have may help."

"All right. Tomorrow after school."

The twins headed for the door. Dan stopped after he opened it, jerking his thumb toward the house. "Oh, by the way, are you finally done using the bathroom now? Other people would like to use it, you know."

"Unless I get to it first!" The two raced to the back door.

***

The Belmont Police Station loomed before Dan and Paul, its brick facade battered by time and weather. The brothers exchanged a glance.

"Ready to do your civic duty, my dear brother?" Dan asked.

"Perfectly. And you?" Paul responded.

"Just as perfect."

They pulled open the heavy door and almost swam through the thick aroma of stale coffee and cigarette smoke that hung in the air as they approached the reception desk.

"Excuse me," Dan said as he addressed the desk sergeant behind the counter. "We're here to see who's in charge of the warehouse fire case."

"Names?" the policeman asked gruffly, not looking up from his paperwork.

"Dan and Paul Case," Paul answered, standing tall beside his twin.

"Ah, the Case brothers," the officer said, finally raising his gaze to meet theirs. "You called in earlier, didn't you?"

"Yes, sir," Dan said.

"Barton is expecting you." The cop jabbed his pen toward a hallway. "Down the hall, last door on the left."

"Thank you," Dan said, and the two made their way down the corridor, bathed in the sterile white light coming from the fluorescent fixtures bolted to the acoustic-tiled ceiling.

Paul opened the door, revealing a cluttered office with walls adorned with various commendations and framed newspaper articles. The detective didn't appear what Paul imagined one to look like. The powerfully built man seated behind the desk was young—about the age of their mother—with black hair and intelligent eyes.

"Detective Barton? I'm Dan Chase and this is my brother Paul. We think we have important information about the warehouse fire," Dan stated.

"Sit down." Barton gestured to the chairs across from him. They complied as the detective slid a thick folder in front of him and flipped it open. "You two were at the fire, correct?"

"Yes," Paul said.

Barton pulled a couple of sheets of paper from the file and reviewed them. "Do you want to add anything to your statements? A description, maybe?"

"No. This is about something that occurred at our home last night." Paul said. "It may have bearing on the case."

Barton leaned back in his metal chair, and the sound of its metallic squeak filled the room. He nodded at them to begin. Paul launched into his story about the intruders who had broken into the twin's house, and how they had stolen Dan's negatives.

"Interesting," the detective said when Paul ended up telling what happened. He turned to Dan. "You didn't take a picture of the arsonist?"

"No, sir. I'm positive I didn't have a negative." Dan grinned at his joke. It fell flat. He cleared his throat. "We thought it was important to tell you what happened. It might have a connection to the warehouse fire."

"Alright," Barton jotted down a few notes on a pad of paper. "Thanks for the information. I'll call the Farmingford sheriff to have him keep an eye on your house, just in case."

"Thank you, detective," Paul said.

"If those two guys approach you again, inform me right away." He folded his hands on the desk and leaned forward. "By the way, I know who you boys are—what you did last summer. Let us handle the investigation this time."

"Uh, yes sir," Paul replied hesitantly, unsure of the detective's tone.

"Thank you for your time, detective," Dan said, standing up with Paul as they prepared to leave.

"Remember, I'm going to keep watch on you," Barton warned as they exited his office. "You two just stay out of trouble—and out of our way."

Once outside the police station, Paul glanced at Dan. "'I'm positive I didn't have a negative?'" He rolled his eyes. "Where did you dig up that little gem?"

"Well, I was hoping the situation would be helped by a little levity," Dan shrugged.

"Very little." Paul took off his glasses and wiped the lenses on the hem of this tee shirt. "Hey, what was with that guy? That 'I know what you did last summer' business?"

"Do you think Dick Tracy the detective in there is jealous because we tracked down and recovered the three hundred thousand dollars Eddie Ridgway embezzled as well as capturing him and the mobster Dalton brothers during our summer vacation and received a ten thousand dollar reward? Do you think he meant that?" Dan asked.

"Yeah, about that."

The twins exchanged glances and shook their heads. "Nah," they said together.

Chapter Five

P aul pushed open the door to Wilson's Hardware Store, the creak of the hinges and jingle of a bell announcing his arrival. The sweet scent of fresh wood and oiled metal filled the air. His gaze swept over the neatly arranged displays of nuts, bolts, tools, and appliances. He grinned when he picked out Betty among them—her jet black hair cascading down her back as she stood bent over, arranging an array of hammers. She glanced up at him when he approached, her face breaking into an inviting smile.

"Good afternoon, sir." She sauntered to him and gave a playful wink. "Welcome to the Wilson Friendly Family Hardware Store. May I be of assistance?"

"You may, young lady." Paul adjusted his glasses and peered around at the shelves. He continued in an overly professional tone. "I'm in need of a pruning saw for my landscaping business. Might you have any suggestions?"

"Why, of course. This way, sir." She matched his formal way of speaking as she led him down an aisle lined with various gardening tools. "We received this one last week." She lifted a shiny saw, handing it to him with a flourish. "Examine that handle, sir. That's craftsmanship. And those teeth... sharp enough to cut through the hardest branches like butter."

"Very nice." Paul ran his thumb down the serrated edge. "But what if I want to cut something... tougher?"

"Like what?" Betty raised an eyebrow and leaned against the shelves. "The male ego, perhaps?"

"Ego?" Paul tried to keep a straight face.

"Ah, yes," she continued. "Ego is a tough substance indeed, particularly the male one, the toughest known on earth, according to science. But I think this saw should do the trick." She tapped the blade with her finger.

"Sold," Paul declared. They walked to the cash register. "You are a superb saleslady, Miss Wilson."

"Thank you, Mr. Case," she rang up the sale. "That will be $1.98."

Paul pulled out some bills and handed them to her.

"Your change, sir." Betty placed some coins in his outstretched hand. "Oh, and we are running a special reward today, but only for our best customers."

"And what is that?"

"Here it is." She leaned over the counter, and they kissed.

Paul stood back, smiling. "That is much better than trading stamps. Only don't let your father catch you doing that on company time."

"Being the owner's daughter has its advantages," she said. The phone rang. With a finger-twiddling wave, she picked up the receiver. "Wilson Hardware."

Paul returned the wave, flashed a grin, and stepped out into the sunlight, the door closing behind him. Leaning against the brick wall, he admired the saw and enjoyed the sun's warmth.

He glanced down the street. A man, whom he had never seen before, came out of a sleek black car and headed towards the store. Tall and broad-shouldered, he wore a sharp suit that seemed more fitting for a Chicago nightclub, but out of place in their small town. What caught Paul's attention was the glint of an ostentatious ring on the man's finger—it all but screamed for attention as it flashed in the sunlight.

The bell above the door chimed as the stranger entered Wilson's Hardware. Paul strained his ears, trying to catch snippets of conversation as the man greeted Betty.

"Good afternoon, young lady." the man's tone was smooth and oily, the ultimate door-to-door salesman. "I'm here to meet with Mr. Wilson about a little... insurance matter."

A knot of unease formed in Paul's stomach. Something about that word—insurance—set off alarm bells in his head. Whistling, he strolled past the window, peering in and watching as the man and Betty exchanged a few more words. Mr. Wilson appeared and guided the man into his office, closing the door.

"Hey, come on!" Dan's voice broke through Paul's concentration, causing him to start. He didn't even hear his twin drive up, dressed in his work clothes. "I've been slinging sundaes all afternoon and I want to get home. Let's go!"

"Dan!" Paul walked over to his brother, his eyes still fixed on the store door as he walked over. "Something's not right in there."

"What's not right?" Dan asked. "What are you talking about?"

Paul gestured towards the shop. "Some guy just went in—a stranger—and he's meeting with Mr. Wilson about some kind of insurance thing."

"Well, insurance salesmen do roam this earth." Dan leaned back in the seat and crossed his arms. "But thankfully, not in packs."

"No, no, this felt... off." Paul stared again toward the store, as though his vision could penetrate the walls and see what was happening in the office.

"Off how?" Concern crept into Dan's voice.

"It's hard to explain." Paul searched to find the correct words. "First off, he didn't look like an insurance salesman."

"How are they supposed to look?"

"Oh, shut up and listen," Paul growled in exasperation. "It didn't sit right with me... his suit was too... too flashy, too gaudy. And he didn't carry a briefcase. He had nothing in his hands, not even a brochure. Then there was that ring the guy was wearing... it could be a lighthouse."

"Alright," Dan said slowly, "but having poor taste in clothes doesn't mean he's not an insurance salesman. He may be in used car sales, though." He waved a hand toward the store. "The guy might just be making a courtesy call. That's why he isn't carrying anything."

"Have you made so many banana splits that the whipped cream has clogged your brain?" Paul snapped. "Think about Mr. Davis." He waited for his brother to put the pieces together. He knew it wouldn't take long. It didn't.

"Wait, hold on… you think that guy in there is trying to pull off a protection racket?" Dan's gesture took in the entire town. "In little ole' Farmingford?"

"You were the one who suggested they may be testing the waters or pulling scams off as they pass through the area, Sam Spade." Paul ran his fingers through his hair. "I don't know. Maybe it's nothing, but if something is happening, I don't want Betty or Mr. Wilson getting caught up in it."

"Okay, then we need to find out what's going on in the office, or if Mr. Wilson and his visitor are only swapping traveling salesman jokes." Dan nodded, his gaze now locked on the hardware store as well. "Let's go around to the back. We might hear something through the window."

"That's got it." Paul eyed his brother's determined expression with relief. When Dan's brain grabbed hold of an idea, it wouldn't let go.

Paul got into the jeep and the brothers drove to the alley behind the store in the block's center. They parked at one end of the alley to make sure their engine wouldn't be heard from inside the office. In silence, they exchanged glances and crept towards the back door, moving like stalking cats.

Paul whispered, "There it is." He pointed to a small, worn window partially open at the top. The two of them shifted along the rough exterior wall, finally pressing their backs against the bricks below the window. They tried to make out the conversation coming through the open crack.

A box fan ran just inside the office, obscuring the words. Even so, Mr. Wilson's anger was evident, although he was keeping his voice low enough not to be overheard in the shop. His visitor sounded cool and collected.

Paul looked at his brother and pointed to his ear in an unspoken question. Dan answered with a shrug.

Mr. Wilson said something that broke off the meeting. The other man offered a sharp reply, and then the office door opened and closed.

Paul looked at Dan and jerked his head toward the jeep. The two crept back and climbed in.

"That was a roaring success," Paul looked at Dan. "Did you hear something?"

"Heard, yes. Understood?" Dan shook his head. "Only a word here and there."

"Great. Now what?" Paul grumbled. "We can't walk in and say to Mr. Wilson 'Oh, we were casually eavesdropping below your office window and that silly fan made it hard to hear what you and your visitor were talking about'."

Dan tossed in, "'Oh, by chance, was it anything about being threatened by a protection racket?'"

The twins were silent for a moment.

"The only thing I got was 'North or Northern or Morton or Something Something Insurance Something'," Dan said. "Sort of."

The brothers exchanged puzzled looks.

"Have you ever heard of a company with a similar name?" Paul asked.

"No. It doesn't sound familiar at all. I guess I picked the wrong time to let my subscription to *Insurance News Monthly* lapse," Dan sighed. "Well, the last 'something' must be 'company' or 'incorporated'. Or 'association'. Something like that."

Paul snapped his fingers. "Wait a minute. The newspaper article... the one about the warehouse. Was anything about insurance mentioned in there? You know, like Mr. Davis was talking about one demanding huge premiums, and the fire was because he refused to pay?"

Dan shook his head. "No. The blaze's cause was described as 'undetermined' and 'currently under investigation', according to the story. No mention of a possible protection racket. They used my picture of Mr. Davis surveying the damage, but not the ones showing the incendiary device."

"Then the cops must be playing this thing quiet." Paul tapped the wheel while he thought. "If they publicized everything they found out about the racket, it could scare the gang away. They would get the jig was up and beat it."

"Well, that would stop any more fires."

"But the bad guys would still run around free," Paul pointed out.

"Yeah. We still have a lot of unknowns here. That guy, poor dresser as he was, maybe from a legitimate firm. After all, we haven't spent our free time memorizing insurance company names. Or he may be from the protection racket. If that's true, Mr.

Wilson won't say anything to us. Remember what Mom told us about what happens to victims if they talk?" Dan ran some options through his mind. "Let's see if there is a legit insurance company name that would fit what we heard. That would be step one. If it's a real one, then we're done. If not, we can figure out what to do next. Let's head to the library after dinner. We'll say we have to work on a school report."

Paul nodded in approval as he started the jeep. "I knew there was a reason I didn't give you to the circus when they wanted you to clean up after the elephants."

The Farmingford Public Library was a generous donation by a philanthropist of questionable character during the late 1800s. Its classical design, which featured white columns and intricately carved capitals, appeared out of place in such a rural area. Magnificent wood paneling lined the reading room walls and a coffered ceiling, now spoiled by the unattractive, modern fluorescent lighting. The twins stopped in the reference section, setting their homework on a table.

"The state requires insurance companies to be registered," Dan said. "I'll check the business directories. You look in the phone books, including the *Yellow Pages*. They may have an ad."

The brothers split up, heading for a different bookshelf, pulling volumes, and returning to their seats. Paul grabbed a stack of yellowing telephone books, each one appearing thicker than the one before. He plopped them all down on the table and began rapidly paging through them, the smell of paper wafting up as he skimmed listing after listing of numbers until his vision grew blurry. After about an hour of searching, Paul closed the cover of the last phone book and blew out his breath.

"Anything?" Paul pulled off his glasses as he rubbed his eyes.

"Nothing so far." Dan's brow furrowed in concentration as he pushed the final business directory away from himself. "It's like they don't exist. Now or ever. You?"

Paul shook his head. "I've checked all the directories up to Chicago. No listings sound even close to our mysterious insurance company."

"Damn," Dan muttered, drumming his fingers on the table. "This is getting us nowhere. We need a new plan."

"Agreed," Paul nodded, gathering the phone books. "But what do we do now?"

"First, let's clean up this mess and shelve these," Dan said. "We might as well do our homework while we're here, then figure out our next move."

"Which is?"

Dan shrugged as he picked up the business directories. "My dear brother, I do not know."

It was at one o'clock in the morning when the idea hit Dan. He bolted upright in his bed. "Of course! How stupid of me!" He threw off the covers, rushed to his brother's room, and shook him by the shoulder. Paul stopped snoring and suddenly lashed out, grabbing Dan's arm. "Down, killer, it's me."

"What the..." Paul let go and sat up, raking his fingers through his hair. "Don't creep up on a fella when he's asleep like that."

"You were sawing so much wood Patton's Seventh Army tanks could have rumbled by and you wouldn't have been disturbed."

"I'll Seventh Army you—"

"Keep your voice down. Don't wake Mom." Dan paced the small bedroom. "Look, we think this North or Northern or Morton or Something Something Insurance Something could be a front for some sort of protection racket, correct?"

"That's what we think." Paul sat up in bed, his arms wrapped around his knees. "But we didn't find anything one way or the other. The North or Northern or Morton or Something Something Insurance Something is about as vague as you're going to get." He flopped back on the mattress. "We could go to the police with what we have."

"We don't have much. Very little, actually."

"Well, they might be able to dig up something we couldn't."

"Remember what Mom told us?" Dan reminded him. "Going to the cops could prove fatal for the businessman who talks. What if the protection racket guys uncover that? Maybe they've got somebody watching the store. Who knows, tapping the phone as well. We don't want to put Mr. Wilson or Betty in danger."

"You're right," Paul agreed. "With no complete name, we have no leads."

Dan sat on the bed. "And now, my dear brother, we come to my brainstorm."

"Will I need an umbrella?"

"You may. We were going about this backward." Dan leaned toward his brother. "We were trying to fit the North or Northern or Morton or Something Something Insurance Something into a pattern of already existing company names."

"And?"

"And we were working the hard way," Dan said. "There's an easier way."

"Well, Einstein, what is it?"

"Simple. Just ask."

"Who?"

Dan stood. "A dissatisfied customer."

***

After school the following afternoon, the twins drove to the Sam Davis Farm Supply warehouse. When they walked in, the proprietor was busy with a salesman, but as soon as he could, he invited the brothers into his private office.

"I'm glad you boys dropped by," he declared. "I didn't feel I had a chance to thank you properly the other night."

"You had a rather narrow escape," Dan said.

"Anything new happened around here since the fire?" Paul asked.

Mr. Davis shook his head. "I haven't had any more trouble, if that's what you mean. I figure whoever set the fire probably assumes the building is being watched by the police."

"The story in the newspaper could have done that," Dan said. "It wouldn't be smart for the gang to try something after that coverage. They could use the article as free publicity... a warning to other victims. An example of what could happen if they don't pay up."

"Are the police watching your warehouse, then?" Paul asked.

The business owner crumpled an advertising circular and tossed it into the wastepaper basket. "No, I asked for a guard, but they said they couldn't provide one. I was told the force is under-manned. Who knows, the commissioner may lack the courage to fight the rackets. Either that, or he's tied up with them!"

"Let's hope not," said Paul.

"Sure," agreed Mr. Davis.

"Most business owners who are approached probably fork out the tribute and keep quiet," Dan said.

"That's it," Mr. Davis said grimly. "They reason the police can't really give them any protection, so it's cheaper to pay a few dollars a week than to have your store wrecked. I know too well."

"Mr. Davis, what was the name of that phony insurance company the gang used on you?" Dan asked. "It wasn't in the paper... along with those other details."

"The detective in charge of the case—" Mr. Davis started.

"Detective Barton?" Paul asked.

Mr. Davis nodded. "He didn't want many details published. That's why the cause of the blaze was labeled 'under investigation' and the incendiary device was not mentioned in the story. So I don't know if I should tell you."

"I suppose it is difficult for the police to get evidence," Dan said. "The other store owners are afraid to testify against the gang for fear of getting rough treatment later on. But we would appreciate it if you told us the company's name."

"Why do you want it?" Mr. Davis asked.

Paul took a couple of steps forward. "Because I think the gang has approached my girlfriend's father, but I'm not certain. If we had the name, we could check if it was real or not. If it isn't, then Dan and I will talk to him. Perhaps report it to the police anonymously to keep him clear of the whole thing."

"That's a big risk," Mr. Davis cautioned. "For everybody involved."

"We know," Dan said, "but we can't stand around and do nothing."

Mr. Davis remained quiet for a long time, surveying the brothers. At last, he spoke. "It is the North Brandale Insurance Company. I've heard of a few people who have taken out insurance with this group rather than risk having their buildings fired. Just gossip."

"Can you give us a list of these people?" Dan asked.

"I could," Mr. Davis seemed reluctant, "but I don't see what it will get you. It might only cause trouble."

"We'll not spread the list around," Paul promised. "But if we confirm this so-called insurance company has also contacted the others, it will help convince Mr. Wilson to go to the police... that he's not alone in this."

"I don't think you'll get to first base, young man," Sam Davis said discouragingly. "But I'll give you the names. Don't let anyone know they came from me."

"We won't," Dan promised. Dan nodded in agreement.

The store owner wrote several names and addresses on a sheet of paper. He handed the page to Paul. "Best of luck." He didn't need to say the next part of the sentence: "You'll need it."

Chapter Six

Outside Davis Farm Supply, the brothers checked the three names written on the list. Since it was getting late, they decided to split up to cover the businesses faster. Paul picked one only a few blocks away.

"Okay. I'll go to the second one," Dan said, "then come back here to pick you up. The third place is between the others. We'll do that one together."

With a mutual nod of agreement and a thumbs-up, Dan and Paul parted ways. Dan returned to their jeep, and Paul made the short walk down the street to the first business on the list: an auto parts store. His nerves raced as he approached the storefront, its windows fogged with dirt. He stepped inside, his shoes sticking to the grime-covered floors as he navigated down the narrow shelves stuffed with labeled boxes and fan belts hanging from the ceiling.

"In the back!" a voice called.

Paul walked toward the rear of the store, where he found a cramped office cluttered with tools and parts catalogs. A portly man in greasy overalls sat behind the paper-laden desk and peered at Paul through narrowed eyes.

"Year, make and model," the man barked out.

"What?" Paul asked.

"The car. Year, make and model of the car," the man repeated in an irritated tone, "for the part."

"I don't need an auto part," Paul answered.

"Whaddya want then, kid?" He went back to the papers. "I gotta finish these tax forms... damn things are a pain in the—"

"Are you the owner?" Paul ventured.

"Yeah. What about it?"

"I'm looking for some information about the North Brandale Insurance Company," Paul said.

The pen the man held stopped for a second, then sped on. "Never heard of them."

"I've been told you can give me—"

The owner snorted, a derisive sound that echoed in the cramped space. He glared at Paul and aimed his pen like a sword. "Look, kid, I don't know nothin' 'bout no Brandale Insurance company. Now if you're not gonna buy anything, clear outta here. I've got work to do."

"Okay, okay, got it." Paul raised his hands. Feeling the weight of the man's gaze, he backed out of the room and closed the door. "Great talking with you. Thank you for all your help."

***

Dan stepped into the fabric store. It was brightly lit and filled with bolts of cloth in every color imaginable. Tucked between two rows of shelves was a small counter. An older woman with lightly curled hair and bright blue eyes that twinkled warmly stood behind it. Her friendly smile invited Dan to come closer, and he couldn't help but feel as if he had stumbled upon somebody's favorite aunt. He half expected her to offer a tray of fresh-baked cookies.

"Hello there! What can I help you find today? We rarely have young men in here." She giggled and lowered her voice conspiratorially. "Don't tell me you sew... or do needlepoint."

Dan laughed. "No, but I am an artist. I mostly do oil landscapes and photography."

"How nice. What do you need?" The woman added apologetically, "We don't stock canvas."

"I was hoping to ask the owner a few questions," Dan said.

"I'm the owner."

Dan grinned. "Wonderful. Have you dealt with the North Brandale Insurance Company? I've been approached by them about a... policy, and I was wondering if you have any information about them."

Her smile faded. Dan could see a shimmer of fear in her eyes as her tone became more stern. "Sorry, but I can't assist you with that. Now, if you're interested in our products, I'd be more than happy to assist you. Otherwise, I have work to do."

"Of course," Dan said. "I didn't mean to bother you. Thank you."

As he left, he couldn't help but wonder if she knew nothing. Her reaction made it unlikely. He grew angrier with the protection racket for targeting her, a sweet lady. He was lost in thought as drove to meet up with Paul. His brother also wore a defeated expression.

"Any luck?" Paul asked as he settled into the passenger seat.

"None," Dan shook his head. "The owner of the fabric store refused to give me any information, but she was scared. Those goons are creeps, strong-arming a little old lady like that. What about you?"

"No soap. I was told in no uncertain terms to get out." Paul raked his fingers through his brown hair. "Let's hope we have better luck in the next place."

They drove to the last company on the list. It was a four-story brick building that dwarfed the two buildings surrounding it and did not try to hide its utilitarianism with fancy frills. The top three floors had single windows at the corners. Alleys ran on both sides of the structure. A bold, painted sign capped the roof: Fenmore Warehouse. The brothers parked and then walked to the door.

"No windows on the first floor either," Dan remarked to Paul. "It may be Dracula bunks here."

Stepping in, they waited to adjust their eyes to the dim lobby. A young woman sat at the front desk, her fingers flying across the typewriter keys. Her hair, blonde and long, was tied back in a ponytail, while her eyes, green and sparkling, looked up at the brothers.

"There's one of his brides. Not bad." Paul said to Dan out of the corner of his mouth.

"Good afternoon, gentlemen. May I help you?" The reception-ist smiled.

"Perhaps you can." Paul flashed one of his charming grins.

The two approached the desk. The young lady gave a little gasp.

"Oh! You're identical twins!" she blurted out, then she blushed. "I'm sorry. I'm sure you hear that all the time. It's just you're the first two I've seen... in real life, that is."

Paul kept grinning. "We are identical, except I'm the more handsome and stronger one." He winked at her.

"In every other way, he's a poor second," Dan tossed in.

The receptionist laughed, a lovely, lyrical one. "How can I help you? Do you need to arrange for some storage? We handle almost everything here: paint, furniture, books, you name it." She looked at Paul out of the corner of her eyes as she twisted a strand of her blond hair around one finger. "I'd be happy to give you a personal tour."

"Perhaps later." Paul smiled again, glanced at Dan, then gave a slight tilt of the head. A subtle, but clear, command for his brother to scram.

Dan moved a few feet to the lobby wall, pretending to become absorbed in a photo of a stack of boxes. He kept one eye on his twin at work in full charm mode.

Paul suavely sat on the corner of the desk. "I really came for some information." He smiled and picked up a letter opener, toying with it in such a way as to make his biceps bulge.

The young lady raised an eyebrow and tilted back in her chair, swiveling it slightly. "Yes?"

"I wanted to ask about the North Brandale Insurance Company. I got a line they've been here lately."

"Well, now, that's a very specific question. Why are you asking?"

"Let's say I've heard some things, and I'm trying to see what it's all about." Paul poured on the charm.

"Well," the receptionist's voice lowered as she leaned forward. "Their salesman has visited a few times, but I don't know much."

"Interesting," Paul mused. "Anything else?"

The young lady glanced around to make sure she couldn't be overheard. "They argued. Mr. Fenmore and that man. Once, Mr. Fenmore threw him out of the—"

The heavy wooden door to the inner office flew open and a burly, middle-aged man charged into the lobby. His arms were thick and his chest broad, suggesting he could lift any crates in the warehouse unassisted. Startled, Paul hopped up, fumbling with the letter opener as it clattered to the ground. He quickly picked it up.

"What's this all about?" the man boomed, glancing between Paul and the receptionist.

"Why, ah, Mr. Fenmore, these gentlemen were inquiring—" the young woman started.

"We were asking about the North Brandale Insurance Company," Dan said as he approached Paul. His brother held the letter opener, still playing with it. Dan gave him a nudge, gesturing towards the desk. With a sheepish grin, Paul returned it to its rightful place.

Mr. Fenmore's manner immediately changed.

"Come in here," he invited abruptly.

The brothers stepped into the office, Paul closing the door behind them. Fenmore stood in front of the two, fists planted on his hips, feet spread apart.

"Look, you tell your boss I already tossed out his other 'salesman' on his—" Fenmore jammed his index finger at the boys.

"No! No!" Dan raised his hands. "We don't work for them! We're trying to learn some information about them."

After a moment, the man sat in a chair behind the desk. He leaned back and stared at the twins. "Why the curiosity about them? People who dig into North Brandale's business tend to end up in trouble."

"We get that picture." Dan stepped up to the desk. "It's just we believe somebody we know has been approached by them."

"That's bad news," Fenmore said.

Paul nodded. "We know, but we're just not positive about it. We're trying to get all the dope we can on the outfit."

"What will you do with the information when you get it?" Fenmore asked.

The brothers exchanged glances.

"In all honesty, we don't know," Dan shrugged, moving next to Paul. "If this person we're... acquainted with admits to being in trouble with this so-called insurance company, we can make plans from there. Perhaps break the logjam somehow. Although I suppose contacting the police may make things worse."

Mr. Fenmore's reply was grim. "Your guess is a shrewd one, young man. For the past three months, a gang that operates under the name of the North Brandale Insurance Company has been shaking down a group of honest businessmen. Those who refuse to take out fire insurance at ridiculous rates wake up to find their property damaged—fires, explosions, goods ruined by stench bombs."

"Can you tell me anything about them?" Dan asked.

Mr. Fenmore shook his head. "Almost nothing. They have no offices or address. The collector who came to see me called himself Mac Slater, but that means nothing."

"Probably an alias," Dan said.

"That's the way I figure it," the warehouse owner said.

"What did this Slater look like?"

"A little better-than-average height, I would say. Broad-shouldered, a flashy dresser. He wears this enormous ring on his right hand. It's really hard to miss," Mr. Fenmore said.

Dan looked at his brother. Paul nodded. "It's the same guy."

"So you have they threatened you, Mr. Fenmore?" Paul asked.

"Yes."

"Have they taken any kind of action against you?"

"They have tried, but I matched them, trick for trick. I didn't fight the German army halfway across Europe to buckle under a bunch of punks here at home!" Mr. Fenmore slapped the desk and got to his feet.

"Have you told the police?" Dan asked.

Mr. Fenmore waved a hand dismissively. "Worthless! I can take care of myself."

"Thanks for the information, Mr. Fenmore," Dan said. "We need more people like you willing to stand up to them."

"With any luck, we can add one more businessman to your side," Paul said.

"Be careful, kids," the owner cautioned as Dan and Paul made their way to the door. "That outfit is nothing to fool with."

***

The brothers stood outside the door of Mr. Wallace's store. Paul took a deep breath, and Dan gave him an encouraging smile. They went inside and walked to the back, their reflections flickering in the glass case holding fishing flies. Mr. Wallace, a tall, thin man with short-cropped black hair, was behind the counter with his back to them as he rearranged a display of irons.

"Mr. Wallace," Paul said.

He turned around and greeted Dan and Paul with a grin. "Oh, hi, fellas. I didn't hear you come in. I'm afraid Betty isn't working today, Paul."

"Yes, I know." Paul fidgeted a little before continuing. "We need to talk to you about something important."

Dan knew Paul could handle the conversation, but he couldn't help but feel anxious about what they were about to reveal. He moved a step closer.

"You're not going to tell me you and Betty are eloping to Las Vegas, are you?" Mr. Wallace laughed.

Paul shook his head and forced a smile.

"Alright, boys, make it quick," Mr. Wallace said, wiping his hands on his apron. "I've got inventory to finish."

Paul took a deep breath. "Have you been contacted by the North Brandale Insurance Company?"

Mr. Wallace's eyes danced nervously between the twins. "What's it to you?"

"Because we've checked. There's no record of them being an actual insurance company." Dan watched the older man closely. Mr. Wallace quickly ran his tongue over his lips. "We've spoken to other business owners who've been approached by the same people, offering the same 'insurance plan.'"

"This outfit seems to have been targeting local businesses in the area," Paul explained. "They're using North Brandale Insurance Company as a front for a protection racket."

"Slow down, kid." Mr. Wallace raised an eyebrow. With a nervous laugh, he attempted a bluff. "You've been reading too many detective novels. Getting as bad as Dan."

"Mr. Wallace, we're serious," Dan's voice held steady despite his nerves. "They threaten violence if the victims don't pay for their so-called insurance."

Mr. Wallace's face paled and glanced around the store nervously before settling his gaze back on the twins. It was clear that their words had struck a nerve.

"Betty told you about the fire. We spoke with the owner, and he said it was started by the gang because he wouldn't give them the tribute," Paul said.

"The other business owners won't say anything, but we think they also have been extorted by this 'insurance' company," Dan said.

"That warehouse was in Belmont, correct?" Mr. Wallace angrily jabbed his finger at Dan.

"Yes, that's right," Dan said, feeling a bit confused.

"And those other businesses? Where were they?" Mr. Wallace interrogated.

"In Belmont, too. But—"

"We're in Farmingford, in case you haven't figured that out," Mr. Wallace shot back.

"Sir," Paul took a swallow and pressed on. "We know about the collector. He may go by the name of Mac Slater... he's a big man who wears a large ring. I saw him come in here."

"Alright, that's enough!" Betty's father shouted. "I don't know where you two got your information, but it's none of your damn business! If I want to get insurance from Adolf Hitler, that's my affair! You get me?"

"Mr. Wallace, we're just trying to help," Dan protested. "Don't make yourself a target out of pride... or fear."

"Help?" Mr. Wallace scoffed. "I don't need help from two teenagers not even wet behind the ears!"

"You must let us tell the police," Dan pleaded. "Look, we understand what happens if they find out a victim talks. We'll do it anonymously... try to shield you as much as possible."

"Sir, please—" Paul began, but Mr. Wallace cut him off.

"Enough! Who do you think you are, the Hardy Boys?" Mr. Wallace thundered. "Paul! I don't want you around my daughter anymore, putting this kind of nonsense into her mind. Got it, kid? You're a bad influence, constantly causing trouble."

"Hey!" Dan blurted out. "Paul's not—"

"Stay out of it, Dan," Mr. Wallace warned, his voice low and dangerous. "Get out, both of you. Don't you dare tell anybody about this. Not a soul. If something occurs, I'll report to the police the ones responsible—both of you. I'll make sure to tell them myself. How would your mother feel about that, huh? Her two fine boys in jail? What would that do to her career?"

"But we—" Paul tried again.

"Come on, Paul. There's nothing else we can do." Dan grasped Paul's arm, tugging him out to the sidewalk, the door slamming closed behind them. A storm of emotions—anger, hurt—washed over his brother's face. "Hey, it's okay."

"Is it?" Paul's voice was bitter, his fists clenched at his sides. "He just kicked us out like we're the bad guys. And ordering me not to see Betty! We were only trying to help." He lurched toward the door. "I'm going back in there and—"

Dan stopped him. "No, Paul, no. Let's take a break. We need to get home. On the way, you simmer down and think about getting through dinner without Mom wondering what's up."

Paul drew in a long breath and nodded his head. During the meal, Dan occupied their mother in conversation, with an occasional glance at Paul, eating his food while staring at his plate. After finishing the dishes, the brothers went out to their workshop.

When they got inside, Paul stripped off his shirt in a frenzy. He thrust his hands into his boxing gloves with a violent twist and assaulted the punching bag with unbridled rage. Dan understood Paul, how his temper would flare in a spectacular firestorm before quickly playing out, so he ignored his brother's wild outburst. He sat on the stool by his easel and continued to work on his current landscape painting.

The savage rhythm of Dan's fists gradually slowed and then stopped. Dan put down his brush and turned toward his brother. Paul's head hung down, shoulders slumped in exhaustion, sweat glistening on his body as he tried to catch his breath.

"It's not fair," Paul grumbled. "We were only trying to help."

"He's frightened, Paul. Scared to death," Dan spoke quietly. "That's why he acted the way he did."

"I know." Paul went to a corner and slid down to sit on the floor. "That doesn't do any good. It doesn't make it better."

"No, it doesn't."

The two were quiet for a minute.

"Why would this racket target someone like Mr. Wallace? He's not rich," Paul said.

"Perhaps it's random." Dan gave a shrug. "The luck of the draw."

"Some luck." Dan pulled off his gloves.

Dan thought for a second. "Or maybe... maybe they pick people who aren't wealthy? Instead, they go after people whose businesses are their whole lives. They'd be more willing to pay for 'protection' if it meant keeping everything they've built, not having it destroyed." He started to clean his brush. "They must have some way to find that out. I mean, to select a business that meets a certain requirement. They certainly don't walk up and down the street, just knocking on doors. There has to be some method."

"That could be it," Paul nodded. "It could be a mix of both—random targets who fit a profile." He stood and tossed his gloves into an old laundry basket that held his other pair. "We can't let them get away with it. How do we prove it, Dan? How do we stop them? Now what?"

"We have to handle this ourselves... carefully." Dan got off the stool. "It's like defusing a bomb in secret without instructions. One false move and everything blows up. At least we can put as much information as we can find in a pretty package, all tied up with a bow, and drop it on Detective Barton's lap."

"That sounds like a good way to go." Paul got to his feet. "Only just promise me one thing, okay?"

"Anything."

Paul slipped on his shirt. "Next time Mr. Wallace kicks us out of his store, you're the one taking the heat for it."

Dan grinned. "Deal."

Chapter Seven

Paul entered the park, as nervous as if stepping into the dentist's office. His eyes gravitated towards the hardware store across the street. He stopped behind the large fountain featuring a trio of egrets, now green with patina, spitting streams of water from their beaks into a shallow bowl, making a sound that always reminded him of the boy's bathroom at school during passing periods. Most of the time, he thought it was funny, but not today.

He stood, uncertain and waiting. Betty and he didn't have any classes together that day, and she had a cheerleaders' meeting during lunch. But she sent a message through Donna that she wanted to talk.

Paul tapped the toe of one sneaker against the base of the fountain while he waited. After about five minutes, Dan, Donna and Betty arrived and walked up to him. A tense silence hung in the air as they all exchanged awkward looks.

"Donna," Dan hinted, as he tilted his head toward a bench out of earshot. He and Donna moved away.

Betty crossed her arms and threw Paul a piercing glare. "Look, I need to know what happened between you and my dad. He's been acting grouchy the last few days, and then, out of the blue, he ordered me not to see you anymore. I have to understand what's going on."

Paul glanced away from Betty, fumbling to find the right words. He wanted to tell her about the suspected protection racket, but he didn't want to risk her safety or that of her father, but he couldn't bring himself to lie. With a sigh, he settled for an attempted compromise. "We had... a disagreement. That's all."

"That's it? 'A disagreement?'" Betty threw her arms open in disbelief. "About what? The proper paint color for your room? You expect me to believe that's all there is to it?"

"Betty, please," Paul stretched his hands towards her. "I would tell you if I could. But I can't."

"Can't or won't?" Betty challenged.

Paul hesitated a moment before answering. "Both," he mumbled.

"Why not?" Her voice cracked with emotion. "Paul, why are you shutting me out?"

"I'm not!" Paul responded.

"You're not? What do you call this, then?" Betty shot back. She dropped the sarcasm and continued in a quiet but intense tone. "Paul, I thought we were going to be honest with each other in our relationship."

"We have been!" Paul protested.

"I thought we had been. At least until now," Betty said. "Listen, Paul, I deserve to be told the truth!"

"Of course you do!" Paul said. "But... but not now."

Betty looked at the ground. "It's not... you're not seeing somebody else?"

Paul took her hands. "No, Betty, no, I swear, nothing like that. Things are going on right now that I don't want you to get involved with. Please understand. Please... you're going to have to trust me."

Betty gazed at Paul, her eyes glistening with tears. "I want to, Paul, I really want to, but it's hard when you don't know what's going on."

"I know, I know," Paul soothed.

She tightened her grip. "Will you promise me that when whatever it is going on is over, you'll tell me everything?"

"Of course, Betty. I promise." Paul risked a smile. "Scout's honor."

"I hope I can believe you," she said in a soft voice.

She might as well have just stabbed him.

"Betty... yes, yes you can," Paul pleaded.

She met his eyes. "Alright, then... but until I know what's going on, all of it, I'm going to follow my dad's order."

"Betty—"

She took a deep breath. "Paul, I will not see you anymore unless you and Dad patch things up. Please don't even talk to me at school. I hope you can understand. Excuse me, I have to go to work." She turned away from Paul and hurried toward the store.

Dan and Donna sat on the bench, watching the scene unfold between Paul and Betty like a movie with no sound. Dan's brow furrowed.

"It's not going well." He shook his head.

"Dan, what's going on with them?" Donna asked. "What is this about with Betty's dad?"

"I can't tell you, Donna. Honestly, I can't." Dan couldn't make eye contact with her. "It's... complicated."

"Complicated how?" she pressed.

"Look." Dan held his hands out in front of him, as though he could yank the correct words out of thin air before dropping them to his thighs. "You need to believe me. I want to tell you, I do, but I can't. It's just... something's going on that Paul and I are trying to figure out. It's best if you don't know all the details. Please, don't ask."

Donna studied Dan's face, finally nodding. "Alright, I'll trust you."

"One more thing," Dan said, his voice low and serious as he met Donna's gaze. "Can you help me out?" He waited for her to nod. "If Betty seems upset or if anything strange occurs at the store, please let me know."

"Of course," Donna replied, with a puzzled expression on her face. "Why—"

"Thanks," he broke in, giving her hand a small, grateful squeeze. "Betty's left. Let me talk to Paul alone for a second."

"Sure."

Dan walked over and clamped one hand on his brother's shoulder. "Hey, how are you doing, buddy?"

"Great. Wonderful. Never felt better," Paul snarled while he watched Betty enter Wilson's Hardware. "What do you think, pal?"

Dan stepped back, raising his hands. "Whoa there, Tex! Don't bite my head off."

Paul managed a tight smile at Dan. "Sorry. I didn't mean to. I'm... I'm upset."

"Understood." Dan gestured toward the bench. "Donna and I are going to the library to do our homework. Do you want to come along?"

"No, I think I'm going home."

"Do you want to use the jeep?"

Paul shook his head.

"Are you sure there's nothing I can do for you?" Dan asked.

"Yeah," Paul jabbed a finger at the trees. "Shut those damn tweeting birds up." He stalked away.

Donna walked to Dan, her eyes following the retreating Paul for a moment. "How's he doing?"

"About how you would expect," Dan said. "He'll go back to the workshop and beat up the punching bag a bit."

"I hope he's okay." Donna linked her arm through Dan's. "Well, let's get to the library, handsome."

For the rest of the week, Paul's presence in the house was a loose, dark thundercloud, only emitting lightning flashes of grunts and single words. Their mother talked to him—after asking Dan to leave the room—and by the end of the week, his sulky demeanor had somewhat improved. He still carried an air of sullenness, but he at least seemed to be back to his usual self.

Dan was first to the jeep on Friday afternoon when the dismissal bell rang. He had climbed into the driver's seat when Donna ran up, dressed in her cheerleader's outfit.

"Dan, I don't have much time. The team bus is about to leave." She spoke soft and fast. "Something happened. You wanted to know."

"I did, yes. Slow down. What's going on?" Dan asked.

Donna glanced over her shoulder before she went on. "Betty is upset. She said an insurance salesman—at least, that's what he said he was—came by the store as it was closing a couple of days ago. He went into the office with Mr. Wilson, and they started arguing. As the guy left, Betty overheard him tell Mr. Wilson that he'd made a mistake, that he'd be sorry. Something's not right, Dan."

"Anything else?" Dan asked, his voice tense.

"Yes," she replied. "Betty told me her father installed a burglar alarm the next day. Last night, it went off."

"Did something happen? Was there a burglary?"

"No. The sheriff thinks it was a false alarm, but Mr. Wilson is very jumpy and nervous, Betty says." Donna glanced toward the bus.

"Has anything else happened in the meantime?"

"Not that I've heard. I've got to go." With a quick wave, Donna ran off.

A minute later, Paul climbed into the passenger seat. "Was that Donna?"

"Yeah." Dan filled Paul in on what Donna had told him. "Think about it. Mr. Gaudy Ring So-Called Insurance Salesman must be part of the protection racket, as we thought. Mr. Wilson refused to pay tribute, so they're gonna target his store to pressure him. They tried something last night but didn't expect the burglar alarm. That scared them off."

"For the time being, but I'll bet one little ding-a-ling bell won't stop them for long. They'll be back," Paul said. He pounded the dash in frustration. "We can't just sit here and let something happen."

"Yeah, but what? When? The gang won't advertise their next strike," Dan said.

Paul paused a second and went on, his voice determined. "There's only one thing to do. We have to keep watch on the store, starting tonight. And keep doing it until something turns up."

"Absolutely correct, my dear brother," Dan nodded. "We'll stake out the place and wait for anything suspicious. If we do spot something, we call the sheriff and catch those goons in the act. Now for this evening's festivities, how to set this up..." He thought for a moment. "Mom knows about you and Betty."

"Yeah. I told her we had a spat."

"Do you have any jobs lined up for today?"

"Only the Evans lawn."

"Good." Dan tapped the steering wheel as he planned things. "When you finish, it will be closing time at Wilson's. I'll let Mom know you decided to go to the game after work to make up with Betty."

"Mom will be mad that I'll miss dinner," Paul said.

Dan waved a hand. "I'll smooth it over. After you get done, hightail it to the hardware store and find a hiding spot. Keep watch."

"I'll be in the park. It's right across the street and there are plenty of bushes," Dan said.

"Good. I work tonight, so I'll say that Mr. Allen is on one of his spic-and-span cleaning kicks again, so I'll be late getting home. It's not a school night, so Mom won't mind. I'll join you when I get off," Dan said.

"Boy, I hate to lie to her," Paul said.

"So do I, but what else can we say?" Dan shrugged. "Tell her something like 'Ah, Mom, Paul and I are going to stake out a store because we hope to catch some dangerous protection racketeers in the act. Don't wait up'?"

Paul chuckled. "I guess not. We'll see what happens tonight."

Dan slapped the steering well. "The Case brothers are on the case!"

Chapter Eight

D an stared at the clock above the soda fountain, absolutely positive the hands were painted on the face. He finished cleaning up the dirty sundae glasses automatically—pocketing the tips without even counting them—his mind completely focused on Paul. He clicked through his brother's activities: mowing the Evan's lawn, raking it, and then getting into position to watch Wilson's Hardware... Dan wondered if anything would happen before he was able to join his twin.

He concentrated on keeping his head down, resisting the urge to check the time constantly, and plowed through work until the shift was over. After the drugstore closed, he hurriedly cleaned the soda fountain and left, saying quick "good nights" to his coworkers.

The park was only a couple of blocks away, so he decided to walk instead of making a noisy entrance by driving. Returning to the jeep, he removed the apron, cap and silly clip-on bow tie. Next, the white long-sleeve shirt came off, revealing his navy blue tee shirt underneath. He reasoned it would be less noticeable in the dark. His work clothes went into the metal toolbox the brothers used for storage, stowed under the back seat.

He started toward the park, his footsteps sounding unnaturally loud. The streetlights threw eerie shadows on the sidewalk. There wasn't much traffic, so he jogged across the road to the opposite side from Wilson's Hardware. He cast a glance at the store; nothing appeared out of the ordinary.

"Paul? Paul?" Dan called out softly as he passed the fountain. "Where are you, buddy?"

Something sharp poked into his back.

"Yer money or yer life," came a gruff whisper from behind Dan.

"Please, sir, I don't have any cash on me." Dan put up his hands. "Just a pack of gum."

"What flavor, bub?" The poke of the object punctuated the question.

"Tutti-fruity."

"Ah, nobody likes that stuff. Keep it."

Dan turned around and faced his brother. "So I guess nothing has happened."

Paul tossed the stick he held away. "A whole lot of nothing, with a huge scoop of nothing on top, served with a side of nothing."

Dan shrugged. "Let's make ourselves comfortable. We may be here for a while."

They glanced around, finally hiding behind bushes. Hours later, Dan stood and tilted his watch so he could read it by the streetlight. "Well, it's only a little after ten..."

"Down!" Paul grabbed his brother and pulled him back down.

A sleek black sedan slowly cruised past the hardware store, stopping briefly in front before continuing to the end of the block. The car edged around the corner, shutting off its lights at the same time.

"It looks like your plate of nothing may get filled," Dan said.

"Okay, let's split up." Paul peered through the leaves. "The alley runs in the back of all the buildings between Third and Fourth. You take the end on Fourth, and I'll take the one on Third."

"Got it." Dan moved away from the cover of the bushes. He shivered as a cool night breeze brushed his face. Rushing across to the street to Fourth, he slowed to a brisk walk as he passed the radio repair store, before stopping at the alley exit. He caught his breath and pressed himself against the cold brick, slowly inching his head sideways until he cautiously peeked around the corner.

The alleyway was pitch black, its darkness seeming to curl up from the ground like a thick fog. A dog's distant bark punched the air as two figures glided down the far end of the asphalt. They halted outside the back door of the hardware store and unlatched a small box mounted next to it. After several moments of hunching over it, they moved to the back door. A jagged, metallic rattling noise echoed off the walls before they cracked open the door and vanished inside.

Time to call the police. Dan rushed back down the block, trying to be as quiet as possible. Impatiently, he waited for a slow semi-truck to rumble past, then ran across the road for the park. Sweat beaded his forehead as he reached the pay phone booth. He dug in his pockets and he took out his tips, hunting through the coins for a dime.

Somebody barreled into him from the side. The two tumbled down to the ground together, exchanging blows as they rolled and grappled on the grass. Dan's opponent got the advantage, yanking him up by his tee-shirt like a rag-doll before driving a fist into his gut. He gasped in pain and doubled over, only to be pulled upright for a second punch.

Dan saw that his attacker was someone about his age with a wild mop of blonde hair. Recognition flashed across the other boy's face. He drove one final pile driver fist into Dan's stomach and ran away.

***

As Dan jogged off towards Fourth Street, Paul crossed the road in front of the hardware store, walking as though he had every reason to be there. He glanced through the window. No lights were visible from the shop's interior. Turning left, he walked by Midge's Dress Shop when the sound of three car doors opening and closing up on Third Street stopped him. A pair of footsteps entered the alley, while another set walked up the block. Then all was quiet. Paul counted to ten and peered around the edge of the building.

The sedan was parked just past the alleyway in front of the dentist's office. The street extended into a residential area, with only a few windows glowing. No one was in sight, so the last person probably turned on the far side of the building on the next block.

Paul tiptoed up to the car. It was shiny and well-maintained, except for a small ding in the rear bumper chrome. He etched the license plate number into his mind and turned to inspect the dark alley. A slight rustling and murmuring voices drifted from deep within one of the stores—Wilson's Hardware, it seemed to him. He crept toward the source of the sound, each footstep feeling like an eternity.

A door squeaked. Paul ducked behind some garbage cans, willing himself to meld into the shadows, trying to become invisible. The door creaked closed, and footsteps approached. He held his breath, every muscle tense, hoping the pounding of his heart wouldn't give him away. Whoever it was walked by, hugging the far side of the alley, keeping them away from Paul's hiding place. The trash cans also blocked his view, and he didn't want to risk taking a look over the lids.

He dared not move until the echoing steps faded away. Finally, the welcome sound of the car driving off let him stand. He trotted over to the rear door of the hardware store. It was closed, but not latched. He ran to the far end of the alley to find Dan. He wasn't there.

Paul was a bit irritated at the thought that his brother had either abandoned his post or chickened out. He sprinted to the park and spotted him sitting on a bench, bent over, massaging his stomach. His twin looked up as Paul neared the spot.

"I saw those two guys go inside Wilson's, so I came back here to call the cops," Dan answered the unasked question. "I didn't know they planted a lookout. He caught me here." He groaned. "Boy, does he have a killer rabbit punch... make that plural, punches. I may not eat for a week."

"Do you think you can stand? Are you all right?" Paul asked.

"Yeah, fine, I think." Dan stood with a slight grimace. "Did you see what any of them looked like?"

Paul shook his head. "All I saw was the back of a trash can. Nothing else. How about you?"

"Ditto, except I did see the lookout as we rolled around on the grass. Tall, about our age, with a head of blonde hair that must be combed with an eggbeater. It's odd, though."

"What?"

"For a moment, I thought he recognized me. I think that's why he didn't beat into a pulp." Dan noticed Paul's expression. "You know him?"

"No... no. What made you say that?" Paul tried to toss it off lightly. It didn't work.

"You *do* know him, don't you?" Dan accused. "I can see it on your face."

"I told you I don't!" Paul turned to head back to the store. "I want to see—"

Dan grabbed Paul's arm and spun him around. "My dear brother, you're a very bad liar. Who is that guy?"

"Let's—" Paul began once more.

"Just wait for one second there, pal! Somebody tries to beat me up. You know who it is and you're shielding him! Why?" Dan demanded.

"Nobody is shielding anybody, especially not me! Dan... Dan, I *think* I know who it is, but I'm not positive," Paul said. "Listen, I just need to make sure. If he's involved, I won't hold back from you or the police. I promise. Let me take care of it. You have to trust me. Please."

"Alright, Paul, I will," Dan said after a pause, releasing his brother's arm. "We've always been honest with each other."

"And we always will be, but I need a little breathing room just now." Paul gestured to the buildings across the street. "Let's see what they were up to in the store before we call the sheriff."

Dan nodded. "Okay, let's go and take a look."

The brothers went back to the alley, pausing at the box where Dan had spotted the two men. They checked the nest of wiring inside. A small wire with two alligator clips bridged a cut wire in the box.

Dan pointed to the break. "Looks like they jumped the alarm system. That's why it failed."

"Mr. Wilson needs to ask for his money back," Paul said.

Dan and Paul pushed the store's back door open, revealing a dark stockroom. They could barely make out rows of shelves neatly packed with boxes and merchandise. The floor was swept clean.

"Great detectives, we are," Paul nudged Dan. "We forgot to bring flashlights."

Dan glanced down and picked a matchbook off the floor. "What's this? Just what we need. We can use them." He struck a match, and they stepped farther into the room. Dan kicked something with his shoe.

"Look at this," Dan whispered, pointing at a pile of packing material discarded on the floor. "Out of place for a stockroom as neat as this one is."

Paul sniffed the air. "Do you smell that?"

Dan nodded. "Like something burning? Ow!" He dropped the match. "That was my finger." He lit another match.

"No, not that... something else."

They squinted, searching for the source of the smell in the dim light. When his eyes adjusted, Dan picked up a glint of metal. He moved toward it and spotted two irons placed dangerously close together on a wooden shelf, plugged into a wall socket. They were surrounded by flammable packing material. He motioned for his brother to come over. "Paul, come here."

"Are those... irons?" Paul asked as he examined the precarious setup.

"It could be a way to start a blaze. Ingenious," Dan said. "Use what's at hand. Take some irons out of the store stock, plug them in, and pile stuff around them that easily catches fire, then switch them on. They would heat up and ignite the packing material."

"You're right. Darn clever," Paul said. "Let's turn these things off."

Dan blew out the match and slipped the matchbook into his pocket. They unplugged the irons and moved them apart, making sure the heat wouldn't reach anything that could catch on fire.

"Okay, we've upset their little plan for a cozy campfire. I hope they didn't buy any marshmallows." Dan brushed off his hands. "Time to call the police?"

"Anonymously, remember," Paul said. "We can't let those lugs get any idea somebody is helping Mr. Wilson, or he brought in the cops. Oh, I also memorized the license plate."

"I'm glad you're using your head for more than a target for another boxer," Dan said.

"Yeah," Paul drawled like a punch-drunk fighter, "I thinks real good, don't I?"

"Every once in a while."

They went outside, closing the stockroom door behind them, and went back to the pay phone. The two collected Dan's tip money that had been scattered over the grass during the fight. With a flourish, Paul handed a dime to Dan.

"What's the license number?" Dan asked as he stepped into the telephone booth.

Paul told him, and Dan repeated it back. Paul gave a thumbs up.

"Here goes nothing." Dan pulled out a handkerchief from his pocket and placed it over the mouthpiece of the phone. He glanced at Paul with a wink. "They do this in the movies all the time," he chuckled. He dialed the sheriff's office and spoke in a deep, disguised voice. "Hello, Farmingford Sheriff? I'm calling to report a burglary at Wilson's Hardware Store. You better send a squad car to check into it. A car with an Illinois plate 305 876 may be involved. No, I'd rather not give my name." Dan hung up and walked out of the booth.

"Let's wait around until the deputy shows up," Paul said, "just to make sure nobody else wanders into the place."

Dan grinned. "We stopped them tonight, my dear brother."

"This time," Paul replied.

Chapter Nine

Paul stepped inside the YMCA gym, the door creaking shut behind him. His gaze shifted to the far corner of the room, where Jake threw punches vigorously into the air as he shadowboxed. Paul strolled up to him.

"Jake." Paul nodded a greeting.

Jake's arms jerked to a stop. He lowered his fists to his side, surprise flickering across his face. "Uh, hi," he stammered.

"I thought I'd work out. With any luck, I'd get sparring in, too," Paul said as he wrapped his hands with tape. Jake didn't respond. "By the way, did I ever tell you I have a brother?"

Jake shook his head.

"He's my twin... my identical twin." Paul observed the other boy's face. "I usually wear glasses, unless I'm here, of course. That's the way some people tell us apart... the glasses." He leaned against the ropes of the ring. "He's a great guy, Dan is. We're best friends, actually."

"Uh... yeah... that's swell..." Jake shifted on his feet. He turned to leave. "I gotta go..."

"Say, what's the hurry?" Paul quickly moved to block Jake, stopping him with a hand placed on his chest. "I wanted to tell you what happened to my brother the other night."

"Yeah?"

"Somebody started to beat him up. Dan can take care of himself—I've shown him a few moves—but not against someone trained to punch hard, like a boxer. Especially a guy who throws strong gut punches."

Jake didn't seem to know what to say for a moment. "That's a tough break for your brother. What's this got to do with me?"

"Well, here's the strangest part. Whoever it was, he seemed to recognize him, stopped the beating and took off. I'm wondering if it was because the person who attacked him was confused... he thought Dan was me."

Jake's initial surprised reaction melted away. His face set into a mask of steely indifference as Paul's implication sank in. The only sign of emotion was an icy glint in his gaze.

"Were you in Farmingford last night?" Dan asked.

"What? No." Jake gave a derisive snort. "Why would I be in that two-bit town? Searching for the exciting nightlife?"

"The guy last night sounded an awful lot like you," Paul said in an even voice.

"What are you fishing for, a confession? I have no idea what you're talking about. Either you, your brother, or both should have your eyes examined. Maybe your heads while you're at it. It wasn't me!" he spat out. "Look, pal, I don't have a car! I mean, how did I get down to Farmingford?"

"Well, someone could have given you a ride… in a black sedan," Paul suggested, paying close attention to Jake's reaction. For a fleeting moment, he noticed a flicker of anxiety in Jake's eyes before his expression glazed over once more.

Bud came up to the pair. "Hey! You two guys plannin' to talk all night, or are you going to spar some?"

Paul glared at Jake and pulled on his gloves. "Yeah, I'd like to."

Jake returned the challenging stare. "I'm up."

Bud pulled up the ropes and motioned for Jake and Paul to enter the ring. They shuffled into opposite corners, glancing at each other with clenched jaws. Bud rang the bell; both boys moved to the center of the canvas, gloves raised in a fighting stance. Jake took the first jab, immediately followed by a hook from Paul. Their shots came fast and furious, an intense dance of power and precision.

"Hey, Jake…" Paul grunted between punches. "So, did you catch a ride to Farmingford?"

"I wasn't there, I told you." Jake's voice wavered slightly as he evaded another punch from Paul. He threw a powerful uppercut, but Paul blocked it in time.

"Did you go with Ricco and Vinnie?" Paul asked, feinting left and landing a solid hit on Jake's ribs. A quick look of apprehension flashed in Jake's eyes.

"Who?" He dodged Paul's right hook. "Are they friends of yours?"

The bell rang. The punches stopped, but neither made a move to their corners nor dropped their guard, but remained in the middle of the ring, panting.

Paul shook his head. "They're not mine. I know nothing about them... other than I wouldn't want to be employed by them. They're a couple of bad characters. Honestly, Jake, if you're involved with them, get out fast... for your own good."

"If I want your advice, pal, I'll ask for it. Keep your nose out of my business," Jack snarled.

He caught Paul unprepared with a punch to the gut, knocking the breath out of him. Paul lunged at Jake, and the two tumbled onto the mat. Grunts and grumbles filled the air as they rolled around, each trying to gain an upper hand.

The bell clanged three more times futilely.

Paul and Jake struggled to their feet, Paul determined to finish what Jake had started. The two boys fought on, throwing punches that sent the other reeling.

"Paul, Jake, that's enough!" Bud shouted from the sidelines. "Stop! Stop!"

Paul landed a strong left hook, sending Jake to the canvas. Jake held up his gloves in surrender.

"What is wrong with you two?" Bud rushed into the ring and yanked Paul back. "Have you both lost your minds?"

"Stay away from my family, Jake," Paul said, his eyes dark with fury. "I mean it."

Jake didn't respond, simply nodding as he regained his breath. Paul twisted out of Bud's grip and headed for the locker room.

***

The next day, the sun was relentless in its strength, radiating off the Case backyard and glimmering off a sheen of sweat on Dan's forehead. He pushed and pulled the manual lawnmower back and forth. It was mid-autumn, yet summer had made an unwelcome reappearance, apparently as a cruel joke to Dan when it was his turn to mow the lawn. Clad in his swimming trunks and old sneakers, his now discarded tee-shirt was draped over a bush as he worked. He cast a dirty look towards his brother, who lay in the hammock, rocking side to side.

"You missed a spot," Paul called out, tilting the neck of the soda bottle he held at an uneven patch of grass a few feet from where his brother was working.

Dan stopped and wiped his forehead with the back of his hand. "Thank you very much for pointing that out," he forced out through gritted teeth.

"Anytime!" Paul smiled. "I'm merely sharing my observation based on professional experience in the lawn care business, my dear brother."

Dan's glare told his brother what he thought of his observation based on professional experience in the lawn care business. "Then, please, allow me to be helpful as well." Dan pointed to the ground in front of the blades. "Lay down there and I'll give you a haircut."

His twin pretended to consider the offer for a moment. "Mmmm... no. That might not be a good idea. You always take too much off the top."

Dan resumed his chore, pushing and pulling the mower. The blades clanked as they scraped the grass, creating a monotonous rhythm that echoed around him. His thoughts, though, were elsewhere.

Donna had called him last night, reporting Betty told her about the attempted break-in at the hardware store... the one the brothers had witnessed. When she mentioned it, Dan instantly remembered the matchbook he picked up in Wilson's stockroom. He couldn't shake off the feeling somehow it was an important clue to the protection racket, but he couldn't figure out where it fit in. As he turned it over in his brain, at last, a link formed.

"Paul," Dan paused his work for a moment, "I've been thinking—"

"Oh? I thought the grinding sound was from the mower."

"Shut up," Dan said. "I've been wondering about those matches we found."

Paul shifted in the hammock, shielding his eyes from the sun with one hand. "What about them?"

Dan leaned on the lawnmower handle. "About how out of place they were."

"What do you mean?"

Dan collected his thoughts as he walked to his brother. "Do you remember how neat the stockroom was at Mr. Wilson's? Say compared to the one at Mr. Allen's. That drugstore storage room is a complete mess. Searching for what I need there is like treasure hunting without a map, but the hardware store had everything labeled and stored properly."

"So..." Paul shrugged.

"So why matches on the floor? In such a tidy place?" Dan stood by the hammock. "For that matter, there wasn't anything for smokers to use. Like ashtrays or empty cans."

Paul slipped one hand behind his head. "That could be true, but we weren't looking for things like that, remember?" Dan grabbed the soda and took a long swig. "Hey!"

"I'm only doing a favor for you, my dear brother. Downing too much of this stuff will rot your teeth." Dan handed the bottle back, then belched.

Paul rolled his eyes. "What a classy sibling I have."

"And don't you forget it, bub." Dan wiped his mouth with the back of his hand. "All I'm saying is it doesn't seem like Mr. Wilson would allow smoking back there, that's all. The place is too clean."

"Okay, how about this: a delivery driver dropped the matches." Dan critically inspected the amount of soda remaining.

"Well, I don't know about..."

Paul gave a laugh. "What else is there? You don't think the matchbook belonged to one of the arsonists, do you?"

Dan nodded. "That's a possibility, brother mine."

"Yeah, but..." Paul frowned. "Ah, come on, Danny boy, that makes no sense. Why would an arsonist leave such an obvious clue?"

"Maybe they didn't mean to. Or they just didn't care." Dan resumed his chore.

"Didn't care?" Paul scoffed, swinging his legs over the side of the hammock. "Seems like a pretty stupid move for criminals who, and mind you, I'm taking a wild guess here, don't want to be caught."

"They could be cocky, like some boxers I know." Dan started cutting the grass again, then stopped, glancing at his brother. "They could think they're untouchable. On the other hand, why should they care about leaving matches? They would've burned up in the fire, anyway. Poof! There goes the evidence in a puff of smoke. Or, who knows, the matches just fell out by accident, and they didn't notice. Things like that happen."

"True, but so what? It's only a matchbook. What can it tell us?" Paul drained the soda bottle.

"It still may be a clue, although we need to work out what it means." Dan resumed his chore, but his mind was still on the puzzle. He kept trying to solve it by relentlessly examining the problem from different angles, even ignoring the sweat dripping on his face.

"Any coffee percolating in the pot yet, Einstein?" Paul asked after a few minutes.

"That's a lousy line of dialogue, but unfortunately, no. I'm going to find out, though." Dan abruptly abandoned the mower in the middle of the lawn and headed toward their workshop.

"Hey! You're not finished here," Paul called after him.

"Later. I want to check those matches again," Dan said without slowing down. Paul followed close behind.

Going inside, Dan sat at the stool by his art table, while Paul leaned against the doorframe. Dan studied the matchbook for a minute, then held it up. "Class, what is this?"

Paul answered in a little boy's voice reciting in school. "A small cardboard folder containing safety matches and having a striking surface along the bottom, commonly referred to as a matchbook."

"Excellent! A gold star for the complete definition."

"Oh, goodie!" Paul jumped up and down and clapped his hands.

"Get yourself under control." Dan tapped the matchbook. "But this item is also something else."

"What?"

"Advertising."

Paul looked puzzled.

Dan pointed to the cover. "Look at the print on the front: 'La Dolce Vita—Belmont's Finest Italian Dining Experience.' Below is a picture of a platter holding a steaming pile of pasta for those who can't read. Address and phone number handily placed on the back."

Paul gestured for Dan to keep going.

"Let's say you have polished off your plate of a delicious meal at 'La Dolce Vita—Belmont's Finest Italian Dining Experience'. You fire up your after-dinner cigar with a match from the complimentary book. You stick the matchbook in your pocket, and every time you reach for a light, you see the miniature ad in your hand," Dan said. "It jogs your memory about the wonderful food. You return, and tell your friends about it."

"I seemed to be saying this a lot today, but... so what?" Paul put his fists on his hips.

"So whoever dropped this matchbook could have eaten at La Dolce Vita. The markets don't sell these things. They're custom." Dan tapped the matches against his lips for a moment, staring off into the distance. "Ricco and Vinnie... those could be Italian names, right?"

"They certainly aren't Swedish."

Dan tossed the matchbook on the table and leaned toward Paul. "What if they're regulars there or something?"

"Come on, Dan, just because their names may be Italian doesn't mean they eat at Italian restaurants all the time. It could be they went only once. Or they might have gotten the matches from another diner," Paul suggested.

"True," Dan said, rubbing his chin as he considered his brother's words. "But that's a lead. And right now, it's the only one we've got."

"Is it?" Paul shrugged. "The whole thing is held together with spit and chewing gum, wrapped up in a bunch of assumptions."

"Such as?"

"Such as! How about these?" Paul counted off on his fingers. "One, the matchbook belongs to the arsonists. Two, the arsonists are Ricco and Vinnie. Remember, neither of us has seen them clearly. Three, Ricco and Vinnie have eaten at La Dolce Vita. Four, they are constant customers at said restaurant. Five, if they are, how do we uncover that fact? Six, if we do and they are, then what?"

"Since when have you become a member of the Quiz Kids?" Dan hopped off the stool and poked his index finger into his brother's chest. "You know, it's people like you who ruin mystery stories for the rest of us."

"Consider it part of my brotherly duties." Paul bowed. "You're welcome."

"I wonder if I could book you on a one-way voyage to the Island of Lost Boys." Dan paced the length of the room in frustration several times. Finally, he made a fist and slugged Paul's punching bag. "Ow!"

Paul grinned. "Not as easy as it looks, huh?"

"You can say that again." Dan flexed his hand.

"Not as easy as it looks, huh?"

Dan rolled his eyes and then sucked his knuckles for a second. He snapped his fingers and strode back to Paul. "Wait a minute. Assumptions can be correct or incorrect. And the only way to determine the accuracy of an assumption is by testing it like you would a scientific hypothesis. And discovering the truth or falsity of one of the assumptions you listed could influence the others as to their validity, correct?"

"Correct."

Dan whirled around. "Therefore, if we can find out more about La Dolce Vita, maybe we'll uncover a way to discover if Ricco and Vinnie are regular customers, correct?"

"Correct. So you are suggesting..."

"If they are regulars, an anonymous message could be slipped to Detective Barton that Ricco and Vinnie might be persons of interest, particularly if they happen to drive a black sedan with a specific Illinois license plate number, which a helpful citizen reported to the Farmingford Sheriff's office in connection to an attempted arson job at Wilson's Hardware. Furthermore, Detective Barton will be told the suspects could be picked up at a specific restaurant they regularly patronize, correct?" Dan stood in the center of the room, staring out the window as he thought.

"Correct," Paul said. "Aren't you going to grill me where I was on the night of January 14th?"

"I happen to know, and your secret is safe with me." Dan turned to his twin.

"So, how do you plan to find out if Ricco and Vinnie are regulars at the restaurant?" Paul asked. "Get jobs as busboys or something?"

"I don't know, I don't know..." Dan stared at the floor as if the answer was written there. Seconds later, he raised his head, a grin spreading across his face. "Of course! A fine dining establishment!" he exclaimed after a pause. "La Dolce Vita calls itself a fine dining establishment." He pushed Paul to one side as he left the workshop. "Out of the way, kid, ya bodder me."

Dan jogged to the house and bounded up the back porch steps. Pushing open the door, he hurried to the living room, Paul close behind. Their mother sat at a small desk in the corner, working on a report for the water department. She smiled as she laid down her pen and looked up at the boys.

"That was fast. Is the grass mowed?" she asked in a tone implying she already knew the response.

"Well, not exactly all of it," Dan said.

"I just put some brownies in the oven," Mrs. Case hinted.

"Double fudge?" Dan asked eagerly.

"Double fudge," Mrs. Case said with a nod.

Paul elbowed his brother. "I think Mom is saying in her own subtle way that the lawn needs to be all cut and raked before you get to chew a mouthful of a double fudge brownie..." He leaned into Dan, "When they come out of the oven... warm... gooey... bursting with all that chocolaty goodness... alongside a nice, tall, cold glass of milk..."

Dan turned to Paul. "You've got a cruel streak, do you know that?" He grabbed the telephone book. "I'll finish the grass, Mom, after Paul and I check something."

The two went back to the porch and sat on the steps. Dan flipped the directory open to the Yellow Pages.

"Restaurants... restaurants..." he said to himself as he flipped through the listings. "Ah-ha! Here!" He pointed to an ad. "La Dolce Vita–"

"Belmont's Finest Italian Dining Experience," the twins completed together.

"Just as I thought," Dan said. "See? Right there. Printed above the phone number."

"'Reservations suggested'," Paul read.

"Which means there must be a list, or a calendar, to write them down." Dan closed the book. "Probably kept at the front of the dining room. That's where they usually are. If Ricco and Vinnie eat there, their names would be on the list. First *and* last names, perhaps."

"Okay, I'll buy that." Paul spread his hands. "How are you going to get a peek, Sherlock?"

Dan's fingers drummed on the directory as he thought. Fragments of an idea formed, and a wide smile appeared as everything fell into place. He nodded. It could work.

"Ah, ah, ah. You've got that look." Paul waggled a finger at his brother. "You've got something up your sleeve. Assuming you were wearing a shirt, that is."

The telephone rang. In a moment, Mrs. Case called out, "Dan! Donna's on the phone!"

"Perfect timing. Coming!" Dan grabbed the phone book and went inside. Placing the directory on the desk, he picked up the receiver and covered the mouthpiece. "Ah, Mom..."

Mrs. Case got up. She smiled and winked at her son. "I think I'll check the brownies in the kitchen."

"Thanks, Mom."

She mouthed "the grass" and left the room. Dan held the phone to his ear. "Hello?"

"Hi, handsome. Betty told me something else," Donna's voice crackled over the wire. "The front window at the store—the big one that faces the street—got smashed by a brick yesterday."

Dan stood up straight. The protection racket must be changing its methods. "That's too bad."

"Yeah. When she went to work, she ran into that insurance salesman—the one I told you about—coming out of the store."

"Okay, if you say so, handsome," Donna said. "Let's go."

They stepped inside the restaurant. The dining room was small, packed with round tables covered in red tablecloths, gleaming silverware, and wine bottles slathered in melted wax from the dripping candles they held. Black and white photographs of Italy decorated the walls: pictures of mountains and fields, lush vineyards, tall steeples and barrel-tiled roofs dominating the landscape. Sounds of clanking pots, accompanied by bursts of Italian, came from the kitchen on the far side of a metal swinging door.

A short, plump, balding man with a huge mustache bustled out of the kitchen carrying a case of wine. He spotted Dan and Donna. He put down the crate and spread his arms. "Saluti amici! I am sorry, we do not open for dinner until four pm."

"While we would love to eat here, we have a different reason for coming." Donna handed him the school newspaper. "We are from the *Farmington High Weekly Bruin*. We are starting a regular column called 'Special Places for Special Dates'. We want to highlight the many fine restaurants in the area for those extra special occasions, like birthdays or prom nights. Not only that, but we'd like to feature La Dolce Vita in a future article."

The man grinned. "Che meraviglia! I am the owner, Domenico Bruni, at your service." He gave a polite bow.

"Oh, that's wonderful!" Donna exclaimed. She turned to a blank page in her notebook, pen poised. "May I ask you some questions?"

"But of course!" boomed Mr. Bruni.

"How long has this restaurant been open?"

"I am the third-generation proprietor!" Mr. Bruni beamed and swept one hand to a wall of photos. "Come, allow me to show you my grandparents. They opened the La Dolce Vita when they emigrated from the old country."

"I'd love to hear about them. Oh, can my photographer take a few pictures of your dining room?" Donna smiled again.

"Take all you please, young man," Mr. Bruni said to Dan. He guided Donna to the family pictures. "Now, here is my grandfather..."

Donna and Mr. Bruni moved away, while Dan snapped a picture of the dining room. He then maneuvered around, raising and lowering his camera, pretending to be searching for the ideal composition. Eventually, he settled by the lectern near the entryway. The reservation book lay on top. He glanced at Donna and Mr. Bruni. They both stood on the opposite side of the room, their backs to him.

"Yes, I'd love to see the kitchen!" Donna threw a glance toward Dan and winked. She and Mr. Bruni stepped through the swinging door, leaving Dan alone in the room.

He opened the notebook. Judging by the sheer number of names written for reservations, this must be a very popular eating spot. Dan flipped through the pages, running his finger down each page as he skimmed the reservations until one name caught his eye: Ricco Toccini... party of two.

"That is fascinating!" Donna's voice from the kitchen was an obvious signal. She and the restaurant owner entered the dining room. "I never knew making tortellini was so complicated!"

Dan closed the reservation book and squatted down, taking a lower-angled shot of the room. He had just straightened up when Donna and Mr. Bruni came up to him.

"Did you get everything you needed?" Donna asked Dan.

"Yes. I got some great shots," Dan replied.

"Meraviglia!" Mr. Bruni turned to Donna. "Now remember, you bring that young man of yours in to dine! The meal I will prepare for you two..." He kissed his fingertips.

Donna smiled. "Well, honestly, he's not very sophisticated. He's more of a burgers and fries kind of guy." She faced Dan. "You know my boyfriend, Dan. Isn't that true? He's kind of basic."

"I think he is quite handsome, debonair and suave," Dan said.

"Obviously, you must be thinking of someone else," Donna commented dryly.

"Ah! You bring your giovane uomo in here, and I shall educate his taste buds with Pork Ragù Over Creamy Polenta," Mr. Bruni confided to Donna.

Donna extended her hand. "Thank you so much for your time, Mr. Bruni. You have been most kind."

Mr. Bruni took her hand and planted a kiss on it. "It has been my pleasure. Arrivederci!"

Dan and Donna said goodbye and returned to the sidewalk.

"Not very sophisticated, am I?" Dan complained. "Why, I can tell the difference between a cheeseburger and a plain hamburger blindfolded!"

Donna laughed. "Well, you take me to La Dolce Vita one night and prove me wrong!"

"Did you see those prices on the menu? I would be lucky to afford one meatball on my pay." Dan put his arm around Donna's waist. "Thanks for your help."

"Anytime, handsome... debonair and suave." Donna giggled.

"Not to mention modest."

Donna rolled her eyes.

Dan glanced at a newspaper rack as they passed by. A headline in the *Belmont Weekly* jumped out at him. He stopped, fished out a dime, and slipped it in the slot.

"What's in the paper?" Donna peeked over his shoulder.

"Oh, just an article I want to read." Dan pulled out a copy and stuck it under his arm.

After dropping Donna off at her house, Dan drove home and went into the living room. Paul sat in the easy chair, feet resting on the coffee table, reading the sports page.

Dan sneaked up behind him. He rolled up the newspaper he carried and swatted his brother on the back of his head. "Bad dog! No feet on the coffee table! Bad, bad dog!" He nailed Paul a second time with the paper.

"Ow! Okay, okay!" Paul put his feet on the floor. "You're as bad as Mom. How did the gumshoeing go?"

"Successful, but first, here's an interesting bonus." Dan tossed the *Belmont Weekly* into Paul's lap and took the sports section. "Give a look at that. Front-page, first column, article just above the fold." Dan sprawled on the sofa while his twin scanned the newspaper.

"So what?" Paul tossed the *Weekly* on the coffee table. "A small fire at a grocery store in Summerfield."

"A mysterious fire," Dan corrected.

"Oh, come on. There was nothing mysterious about it." Paul gestured toward the paper. "It said a bunch of oily rags burst into flames."

Dan sighed. "How do you keep getting good grades at school with such poor reading comprehension? What type were they?"

"A pile of rags soaked with linseed oil," Paul answered. He smirked. "Poor reading comprehension, huh?"

"And what is linseed oil?"

"I'm sure you're about to tell me." Paul settled back in the chair. "I'm ready. Go."

"Linseed oil is used for finishing wood, and is also mixed with oil paint," Dan said. "If it is present on cloth when it dries, it undergoes oxidation that releases energy in the form of heat when exposed to air. That creates the potential for spontaneous combustion."

Paul cocked one eyebrow. "Impressive. Have you been slipping issues of *Popular Science* between reading *True Detective*?"

"Now observe how I cleverly weave those together." Dan leaned toward his brother. "Why were rags soaked with that stuff at a grocery store? The article didn't mention any remodeling work or painting going on. So how did they get there? Did they migrate?"

Paul was quiet for a second. "Wait. Hold the phone. Are you suggesting that the gang...?"

"Left the pile of oily rags as a calling card? You betcha." Dan spread his arms wide. "Step right up, young man, you win the Kewpie doll."

"But in Summerfield?" Paul sat up. "Isn't that place smaller than Farmingford? Why there?"

Dan leaned back, his gaze contemplative. "Let's say we want to start running a protection racket. We offer so-called 'insurance' against 'accidents' happening. Maybe the customer refuses, so we cause bad things to occur—fires, vandalism, even physical harm—until he does pay up.

If we pick a large city like Chicago, then we'd have thousands of potential targets and, with millions of residents, be able to remain anonymous for the most part. What if we choose a rural location to open shop instead? Well, we could target farms as well as businesses, for one thing. What farmer wants his barn to burn down or his equipment damaged? But if we concentrated our activities in one small geographic area or one town, it's more likely that a rash of mysterious fires or other mishaps will draw attention from local cops."

Paul nodded. "I'm with you so far."

"Okay, what if we try a different approach? We'll spread out. Start by hitting this location first, then move on to the one in the next county, and so forth. Summerfield is in a different county, about two hours from here, and Belmont is an hour north of here. That may be enough distance to make it harder for the authorities to link what happened, but still close enough to drive. Separate police and fire departments might make it difficult for them to work together. What else? Not only do we move things around geographically, but we also do chronologically. Lie low between incidents. Let the excitement die down before striking again. That would keep the victims isolated, confused, and afraid."

Paul was quiet for a moment, then picked up the newspaper to reread the article. "So you think the racket is based in Belmont..."

"With a web spun out over the entire area, and one big fat spider sitting smack in the middle of it," Dan said. "Somehow, he selects who and where the targets are."

"That makes sense," Paul said. "So why don't have the police considered this?"

Dan shrugged. "I'm sure they have. But we're back to the old problem: the victims aren't spilling because they're afraid of reprisals. That's the protection racket's greatest advantage. We need specific information, so the whole organization can be shut down at the same time. Let's say, details provided by a couple of young, concerned citizens concerning the identification of the possible arsonists."

"I'll buy that. What did you find out at the restaurant?"

"One Ricco Toccini has reservations for a party of two the day after tomorrow at 5:30 pm." Dan linked his fingers behind his head. "Ted will take my shift at work, I'm sure. He's saving up for a car. Then you and I will supposedly take in a movie in Belmont... but instead, we'll be watching outside La Dolce Vita."

Paul gave a thumbs up.

Dan grinned and glanced at the clock. "Mom gets home soon. Speaking of restaurants, what's for dinner?"

Paul straightened up, alarm crossing his face. "Dinner?"

"Yes, dinner. The main meal of the day, usually eaten in the evening," Dan said. "It's your turn to cook tonight, my dear brother."

"Shoot, I forgot!" Paul jumped to his feet and rushed into the kitchen. "Where's the can opener?"

***

Dan and Paul sat parked in their jeep on a quiet side street across from La Dolce Vita. Dan finished the last of his burger. He crumpled the wrapper into a paper sack before checking his watch. He reached behind the seat to a metal toolbox. "It's almost time," he said as he opened the box's lid and tossed his trash inside.

Paul took a few more bites of his french fries and then nodded. He clumsily punched his brother in the arm and with a salt-covered finger pointed toward the street. His words came out muffled through the greasy food. "There they are!" he said.

The two beefy men swaggered along the sidewalk. Their black hair was slicked back, and they wore double-breasted pin-stripe suits that stretched tight against their broad chests. They opened the door to the restaurant and stepped inside.

"They fit the part," Dan said. "Are you thinking that's the two?"

Paul spoke through a mouthful of fries. "Vinnie is the lug wearing the loud red tie, and Ricco's in the white one." He swallowed. "I'm pretty sure, but I'd like a closer look to be positive."

"You can see the entire dining room through the glass," Dan said. "Let's stroll past, and you can take a peek. If it is them, we'll continue to the parking lot in the rear to check out what they drove."

They left the jeep, crossed the street, and walked along the sidewalk. As they passed by the restaurant window, Paul casually glanced in and saw the men sitting at a table.

"That's them," he said out of the corner of his mouth.

Dan nodded his head. "Let's look for the car."

The siblings continued walking down the sidewalk, taking a turn at the end of the building. Without any black sedans in sight, they went to the lot behind the building.

Paul pointed. "Bingo... in the last row."

They went up to the sedan. Dan gestured at the plate. "Are you sure this is it? We told the sheriff's department Illinois tags. This pair is for Ohio."

"It's the same model and year." Paul pulled a piece of paper and a stub of a pencil out of one pocket and scribbled down the license number.

"There must be more than one black sedan like this in this area," Dan said. "Or they could drive more than one car."

Paul examined the bumper. "No, this is the one. See that slight ding in the chrome? The one I saw had that too."

"Maybe they have a box full of stolen plates that they switch out after each job." Dan pointed to the trunk. "Let's bug out of here before someone dials the cops because we're snooping around." They began heading back to the jeep. "When those bruisers finish eating, we'll tail them to make sure they return to that black sedan. If they do, we can tell Detective Barton about their tag-swapping routine."

An hour later, Ricco strolled out of the restaurant, a toothpick wedged between his teeth, a satisfied grin on his face. Vinnie followed him, opening a mint and dropping the wrapper on the sidewalk. Dan fumbled for his keys.

"Wait!" Paul stopped Dan. "They're not going back for their car!" He watched the men's progress for a moment. "Where are the heck are they going?"

"Maybe they're out doing a little of window shopping," Dan said, "for a new pair of brass knuckles."

The two men walked a few more steps down the sidewalk, then re-entered the same brick building that held La Dolce Vita, going through a set of double-pane glass doors just past the restaurant's front entrance. The twins exchanged puzzled looks.

"Why are they going in there?" Dan asked. "Are there apartments inside?"

"I don't think so, but sitting here won't get us any answers. Come on." Paul vaulted out of the jeep's open door and crossed the street in a loping run, Dan following. Together, they hurried to the doors and stepped inside.

The two boys found themselves in a small, starkly lit lobby. The floor was a checkerboard of tiny tiles, alternating between obsidian black and what was at one time a pristine white. The walls were painted a plain beige, hardly a color at all. However, a bold black chair rail ran horizontally around the room, breaking up the monotony. A lone plastic philodendron coated in a thick layer of dust, stood lifeless in the corner as the only decorative item in the lobby. Paul's finger traced down the directory of building tenants encased in a glass case. But some letters had fallen out over time, rendering some names illegible gibberish.

"No Protection Racket Incorporated listed," Paul said. "Or North Brandale Insurance Company, either."

"What a surprise," Dan said.

"But there are a lot of blanks next to the office numbers. They must be vacant."

A loud humming filled the lobby. Their attention turned to the elevator. The boys glanced up at the indicator above the door and watched the arrow descend from the fourth to the third floor, and continue slowly downward. Their eyes were drawn to its movement.

"Are those guys coming back down?" Dan asked.

"Seems like a short visit. I don't want to risk running into them here," Paul said, scanning the area.

Paul grabbed Dan by the arm and pulled him towards a door to the side of the room. He twisted the handle, opened it, and pushed Dan through before entering himself and shutting the door firmly behind him. The clicking of the door echoed loudly in the lobby, just as the elevator doors swooshed opening and the gate rattled.

"Made it in time," Paul muttered.

Dan nodded in agreement. The sound of high heels tapped a steady rhythm on the tile floor until reaching the street exit.

"I don't think that was Ricco or Vinnie," Dan said with a grin.

"Let's get out of here." Paul began to open the door, then closed it. He put his finger to his lips.

The sound of heavy footsteps echoed off the tiled lobby floor, causing Dan to freeze. He held his breath as the metal elevator doors creaked open. Paul carefully peeked through the slight opening before quickly closing it again. The elevator groaned as it began its ascent.

"What? Who did you see?" Dan asked quietly.

"The Mr. Gaudy Ring insurance salesman just rode up," Paul answered.

"So he's upstairs with Ricco and Vinnie," Dan said.

"Let's call Detective Barton—"

Dan shrugged. "What would we tell him? We only have a theory and circumstantial evidence—nothing concrete to back it up. What if what we've got isn't strong enough to make an arrest? Or even to get them on the police radar? If the cops get involved too soon..."

"The gang may blow town," Paul finished. "And we'll be done with them."

"That's true, but they might just move their scheming to a new place, where they'd be free to continue running their racket on different people, like you said before," Dan replied. "Not to mention possibly retaliating against their marks here as a parting gift. You know, something to use as a cautionary tale for wherever they end up. Would read great in their brochure."

"Okay, what are we supposed to do in here, Gang Buster?" Paul challenged.

"I'll bet those three aren't sitting in an office playing Parcheesi. It would help if we had names or dates to strengthen our case." Dan thought aloud, tapping his fingertips to his lips. He pointed. "Those stairs may lead to somewhere interesting."

"Downstairs surely leads to the basement," Paul said. "That's probably where the bodies are buried."

"Let's not go down and find out. Shouldn't this staircase go all the way to the building's top?"

Paul nodded. "It usually does. It can be used for emergencies or when the elevator is out of order."

Dan looked at his brother. "We need to hope nobody uses them and the other floors' doors are open."

Paul grinned briefly. "And that nobody sees us go through them. Come on."

Chapter Eleven

"What floor did the elevator stop on?" Dan asked.

Paul peeked out the door. "Four."

"Let's discover what the excitement is up there." Dan bowed and swept one hand wide. "After you, sir."

"Why, think you very much. You are most kind." Paul inclined his head.

The two started upstairs, their hands sliding along the handrail as they climbed. Despite their best efforts, it seemed to Dan their footsteps created an obnoxious pounding noise bouncing off the walls that must have sounded like tiptoeing water buffaloes. They reached the fourth floor and stopped on the landing in front of a heavy door.

Dan wrapped his fingers around the cold, metal doorknob. He twisted it ever so gingerly, relieved when the latch clicked. A sliver of light shone through the gap as he pulled the door open. After taking a deep breath, he widened the crack to check down the hallway. Empty. After a few seconds of reassuring stillness, Dan swung the door wide and stepped through, motioning for Paul to follow him.

They stood in the corridor, the wooden floor covered by a worn red runner that had seen better days. A solitary window marked one end of the corridor, admitting light from the streetlamps outside. The elevator took up the opposite end, its doors shut tight. Fluorescent fixtures hung overhead, washing the walls in a sickly, yellowish glow. Ten half-glass doors were arranged in staggered rows, some displaying fading names in gold lettering, while others bore no markings at all except for a room number. Darkness filled every door except the last one down the hall.

Dan gestured for Paul to stay put, and then he crept down the hallway, remaining in the center of the carpet. A floorboard gave an unexpected, loud squeak. He froze, perched on one foot, arms out to his sides, looking like some type of odd wading waterbird. No response came from inside the office, so he continued.

He edged his way towards the door with a dim light illuminating the glass and spilling out from its slightly opened transom. The name "Murdstone Inc." was freshly painted on the glass.

Dropping to his knees so his shadow wouldn't show, he peeped through the keyhole. It was blocked. He pressed his ear against the door. Indecipherable voices came from the other side. After listening briefly, he glanced at the transom and gestured for his brother to come.

Paul walked to Dan, trying to avoid any creaking boards. Dan took hold of Paul's arm and directed him towards the door. He cupped his hands while tilting his head towards the transom. Paul understood and linked his own fingers together to provide a step, then nodded when he was ready.

Dan planted his foot in the cradle formed by Paul's hands and grabbed hold of his brother's shoulders for stability. With careful, steady pressure, Paul hoisted Dan off the floor. Dan kept one hand pressed against the wall to prevent him from making any noise from bumping or scrapping into it.

Dan gripped the doorframe, leaned in, and peered through the narrow transom opening. He turned his head, trying to see as much of the area as he could.

All he saw was a small, dim waiting room of a two-room suite. It only contained a sofa and a small secretary's desk, its surface completely empty of papers, a typewriter or a telephone. A slice of light, along with murmuring voices and laughter, filtered through another partially opened door leading to the inner office.

The whine of machinery startled him for a moment, but an instant later he recognized it as the sound of the elevator descending. Paul didn't wait for Dan's frantic "down, down" signal before lowering him to the floor. The two scurried back to the stairwell, where they could talk in relative safety.

"Well?" Paul whispered.

"Murdstone Incorporated doesn't spend any money on interior decorations, I can tell you that much," Dan said. "The corridor door opens into a waiting room that looks like it's never used. I mean, it has no magazines, no pictures, nothing. The secretary's desk is completely bare... not even a phone."

"Maybe it's a branch, and doesn't need to be fancy," Paul suggested.

"Or it's a front," Dan replied. "A fake business setup that allows the protection racket to have a safe location to meet—their headquarters."

"Well, given who's in there now, that makes sense," Paul said. "Could you hear what they were talking about?"

"No. I only heard what sounded like three guys shooting the breeze," Dan shrugged. "They were all in the office beyond the waiting room. Unfortunately, I couldn't make out exactly what they were saying."

Their conversation stopped as the elevator shuddered to a halt behind the wall enclosing the stairs. The doors moaned open, then metal gates rattled open and slammed shut again. A moment of silence followed before determined, precise footsteps, sounding almost like marching, echoed down the corridor. A door opened and closed down the hall.

"I don't think that was the pizza being delivered," Paul remarked.

"No, but I wonder if it was a big, fat spider heading for the center of its web," Dan said. "Man, I'd like to know what's happening in that office."

"So do I, but we can't hang around in the hallway or use the transom again. We don't know if more guests are coming to this little party," Dan said.

"True." Dan thought for a second. "Wait..." He slightly opened the door and gestured towards the window at the hall's end. "If there's a fire escape outside, there's probably a platform running across the whole building. If I could climb onto that, I could peek in from the outside. At least I could catch a glimpse of them, maybe the big boss. Boy, I wish I had brought my camera."

Paul grabbed his arm. "Using the window on this floor is risky. It's right next to the office."

"I know." Dan drummed his fingers against his cheek, then stopped. "I'll go down one flight. There's probably a window there, too. I just climb out and go up by the fire escape. You stay here to see if we have any late arrivals."

"Check."

Dan moved down the stairs, his feet barely making a sound. He stepped into the third-floor hallway and glanced both ways. The corridor was the same, except for different titles on the doors. Every office was quiet. Nobody working overtime in this joint.

He jogged to the end of the corridor and peered through the glass. Dirt covered it, but he could see the iron railing of the fire escape outside. He flipped the latch, grabbed the two sash handles, and strained with all his might to raise the window. It wouldn't move.

Gritting his teeth and groaning with effort, he tried a second time. But the window remained firmly in place. He checked the bottom of the sash and discovered why: it was painted shut.

There still may be a chance, he thought. Every floor must have a window like this, and one of them must work. He hoped.

He went to the second floor, walked to the window, and gave it a tug. It, too, would not budge. Growling in frustration, he hurriedly headed back to the fourth floor, climbing two steps at a time.

"They're stuck. Both have been painted shut," he told Paul, pointing downstairs. "Great emergency exits."

"I'll remind you to report this landlord to the fire marshal," Paul responded.

"I'm trying floor five. Last chance."

Paul nodded, and Dan bounded up the concrete stairs. The fifth-floor hallway was quiet as death as he stepped into it. Silently, he approached the window and gripped the handles with his fingers. With a gentle push, it remained stubbornly in place. He swore under his breath, then gathered all his strength. Another thrust upward again. The sash protested, then gave way with a satisfying whoosh.

The cool night air rushed into the hallway and brushed past his face as he leaned out. The fire escape was bolted onto the brick exterior of the building. Dan grabbed the iron railing and shook it. It appeared solid enough.

He had one foot on the sill when he stopped, realizing the corridor lights would make his exit visible to anybody who happened to pass by. He didn't want to be reported as the friendly neighborhood cat burglar to the police. Quickly striding back to a switch on the wall next to the stairwell door, he clicked it off. The hallway went black.

Dan returned to the end of the corridor and stepped out onto the metal platform, leaving the window open. He looked over the railing, checking the empty side street below that split the restaurant from its neighboring block. No one was in sight, and the building opposite was dark. Traffic sped by on the avenue, while dishes clattered in the restaurant kitchen, breaking the stillness of the night. Glancing up, he noticed the fire escape extended to the rooftop.

Taking a deep breath, Dan moved slowly down the steep ladder. The whole contraption vibrated, and he halted, glancing at where the fire escape was attached to the bricks. Convinced the bolts were still in place, he continued down to the platform, trying to make the steps rattle as little as possible.

Dan made it to the fourth floor. He stepped up to the window and looked inside. Paul poked his head out from the landing door.

Voices and footsteps echoed from the street as two men stopped at the corner. Dan understood he was silhouetted by the hall lights just as on the floor above. He didn't want the men to look up and spot him skulking there like some cheap, two-bit thief.

Paul still looked down the corridor. Dan stooped and waved at him. Once he got his brother's attention, he jabbed his finger at Paul, then at the overhead lamps several times. After a few moments of confusion, Paul figured out what Dan meant. He checked the switch behind him before giving a thumbs-up. The hallway plunged into darkness. Dan remained as still as possible.

From the street corner came the familiar sound of a match being struck. A tiny flame flared up, illuminating the two figures as they lit their cigarettes, talking and laughing between puffs. *Aw, come on, hurry it up, you guys,* Dan thought.

The cigarette ends glowed as the men continued their conversation. Finally, they flicked their smokes into the gutter, a tiny burst of sparks erupting as the butts hit. With a wave, one figure walked east and the other west.

Dan stayed crouched on the platform, listening to the sound of the men's footsteps echoing down the street and fading. The world beneath his feet returned to darkness and quiet. Dan exhaled for the first time in what felt like hours.

The window gap was big enough for Dan to wiggle through without risking having to move it. He contorted his body and squeezed inside, then stood upright and took a few moments to stretch out. Moving to the door, he pressed his ear against it. Again, it was a complete waste of time. He couldn't hear any better than he did before; only the murmur of voices reached through the door, but not any clear words,.

Dan went back to the fire escape, frustrated. If only he could hear something, or see something, that would be of use... He gazed at the window of the office, a luminous square in the darkness which both beckoned and mocked him at the same time.

With a sigh, he ruffled his hair with his hand. Looking down, he spotted a foot-wide granite ledge, covered in bird droppings, that accented each floor of the building.

"It's only about ten feet over to that window," Dan mumbled to himself. If listening at the door failed, time to try the window. He climbed over the fire escape railing. "This is stupid, stupid, stupid."

Pressing his face against the wall, he stepped onto the stone and clawed his fingers into the mortar between the bricks. His heart beat wildly as he inched closer to his goal of the illuminated window. He slid his right foot, then left foot, then repeated, step by step, inch by inch. Beads of sweat formed on his forehead as he feared what would happen with a misstep.

A gust of wind roared through his hair, threatening to knock him off balance. He could practically hear the sickening splat he'd make if he plummeted from the fourth floor. Against his every instinct, he forced himself not to look downward. He repeated in his brain the mantra of "don't think about it" as he scolded himself for even entertaining such thoughts. Time to move on.

Right foot... left foot... right foot... left foot...

A piercing blast from a car horn echoed down the narrow street. Startled, Dan gasped and tipped backward, his balance upset. His heart was pounding as he clutched at the wall and threw his body forward to keep upright. He stayed still for a moment, his face pressed against the cool surface of the bricks as he caught his breath.

He swallowed and resumed his journey: right foot... left foot... right foot... left foot...

When he finally arrived at the window, he had to stop shouting in triumph. He grinned. Piece of cake!

The grimy glass made the people in the well-lit room look blurry. Dan needed to avoid getting too close to the panes themselves to help prevent him from being seen by the men inside. Taking a firm grip on the frame, he peeked around the edge of it.

The office, like the waiting room, was barren. It only had a desk and a tall-backed swivel chair facing away from the window. A lone file cabinet—Dan wondered if it was empty, like the rest of the furniture—occupied one corner. There was nothing on the walls—no prints, no calendars, no charts, no nothing.

Ricco and Vinnie were seated next to each other on two metal chairs, their arms folded across their chests as they listened intently to the person speaking from behind the desk. The insurance salesman was leaning against the nearby filing cabinet, also focused on the same individual. Although Dan couldn't see who sat in the chair, every so often a hand would appear and gesture while making a point. It was evident to Dan that the individual behind the desk held all the power, the large spider controlling a protection racket web.

Dan held his breath, willing himself to catch the slightest whisper of conversation. He strained his ears, but all he could make out were words and fragments of sentences that made no sense. His mouth drew into a thin line, and he leaned forward still more, desperate to understand what was being said.

The four were engrossed in an intense discussion. The man behind the desk slid a paper across to Ricco and Vinnie. They read every line before handing it to the insurance salesman, who scanned it, nodding as he did. They must be discussing plans for their next targets, Dan decided.

The man at the desk pushed some cash towards others in the room. Carefully, he divided it into three piles and moved each one to its intended recipient. Ricco and Vinnie examined their stacks closely, holding the twenty-dollar bills up to the light to ensure they were authentic. Satisfied with their share, they tucked the money into their pockets.

Suddenly, Vinnie jumped up from his chair and approached the window.

Dan's muscles froze. He told himself *Freeze!*

He had no choice but to do it. The shadows and dirt of the window should still conceal him, and he might be able to remain unseen—that is, unless he betrayed himself by moving. Dan forced himself to stay still, keeping every part of his body motionless.

Vinnie didn't turn his head to look at the glass pane where Dan was peering through, as he said something to Ricco. While he continued to talk, he reached behind him with one hand and yanked on a drawstring, pulling a thick dirty beige blind down to cover the window. It was just as effective as a brick wall in blocking prying eyes.

Dan stared at the window shade, and he let out his breath in relief that he hadn't been spotted. Like a comedy movie, the shade unexpectedly sprang up with a loud thwack, its cord coiling and looping rapidly.

Vinnie reacted with lightning speed, pivoting on his heel and lunging forward to grasp the cord. He cursed as it darted away from him, then leaned closer still with eyes narrowed in determination as he studied the window shade cord's swinging arc. His grip closed around the ring at last, and he grinned in triumph.

And then his eyes stared directly into Dan's.

The two of them looked at one another, separated only by a thin pane of glass, their faces mere inches apart. After a few seconds, Dan congratulated himself once more: Vinnie hadn't spotted him.

Then Vinnie shook his head in disbelief and blinked, almost as if he were trying to convince himself that it was his own reflection staring back at him. He jerked back from the glass, his mouth opened in surprise. Vinnie turned back to the others and pointed. For the first time that night, Dan heard and understood what was said from inside the office. "Hey! There's a kid out there!"

"Go, go, go!" Dan muttered to himself and started to retrace his steps as fast as he could, eyes fixed on reaching the comparative safety of the fire escape.

His heart pounded as he continued inching his way along the narrow ledge of the building, hands brushing against the rough brick wall. He was about halfway to the platform when moving too fast, he slipped on some bird dung. Losing his balance and tipping backward, he lunged desperately for a grip, but couldn't get a hold of the bricks. His feet slipped off the ledge and into space.

Chapter Twelve

Paul leaned against the wall of the stairwell and checked his watch again. What was taking his brother so long? He absentmindedly tapped his foot on the concrete floor, his eyes darting around in boredom. Sighing, he took off his glasses, slipped them into his pocket, and rubbed the bridge of his nose. Every few minutes, a clank of crockery from the restaurant would break through the silence, startling him and putting him on edge.

A commotion erupted from the end of the hall.

"They must have spotted Dan!" Paul said out loud. His mind scrambled for a plan, and his protective instincts took over. He clenched his jaw and the muscles in his arms tightened as he flung open the stairwell door and pounded down the corridor.

Ricco, Vinnie, and Mac, the insurance salesman, boiled out of the office like angry hornets from a nest. Paul couldn't fight off all three of them, but he could distract them. It would give Dan a chance to escape if he had to. He stopped, making sure they spotted him.

"That's him!" Vinnie pointed at Paul. "He must have slipped through the window!"

"Get him!" Ricco yelled. "He may know too much!"

Paul spun and sprinted down the hallway, the thundering steps of the men behind him growing closer. When he reached the door to the stairs, he chanced a quick glance back and caught sight of the insurance salesman lagging behind the others. Mac was panting, clearly struggling to keep up with the chase.

"Nice try, pal. Time to lose some weight," Paul said under his breath, smirking at Mr. Gaudy Ring's futile attempt to be intimidating.

"Hey you, kid, stop!" Vinnie's voice dripped with menace. "We just want to talk with you!"

Over my dead body, Paul thought as he burst through the stairway door. His feet pounded against the steps with the force of a pile driver, reverberating between the walls like thunder. He threw himself into each turn of the stairs, using the newel posts to vault around every corner to stay just ahead of pursuers.

Paul reached the first floor while the others were still out of sight. Suddenly, an idea struck him. He pulled open the lobby door with a loud bang, then made for the basement door. When he reached the cellar steps, he swung over the single metal railing near the top, nearly stumbling, but regained his balance just in time. He swiftly dove between two pillars beneath the stairs, pressing his body tightly into the shadows. Within seconds, he heard the others reach the landing above.

"Where did that little punk go?" Vinnie skidded to a halt.

"He must've left through the lobby," said the salesman, still panting. "The door's ajar. I'll check." The door slammed open as he rushed through. He returned in a minute. "Nothing, not a trace of him outside."

"That means he's still in the building." Ricco's voice was cold and calculating. "We search out the whole place, got it? Mac, you guard this door. Lock the outside glass doors and turn off the light. This place is closed for the night. Make sure nobody uses the elevator, except the boss. Vinnie and I look for the snooper."

"What if the kid shows up here?" Mac sounded worried.

"He's a kid! You got a gun," Vinnie said.

"But the boss said no noise," Mr. Gaudy Ring reminded them nervously.

"Well, hit him with the gun butt! Cover him with it! Do what you have to! He doesn't know what our orders are," Ricco said in exasperation. He went on in mock politeness. "We simply wish to chat with him. That's all."

Vinnie's chuckle was ominous. "We don't need no firepower for that. We have ways. The person either talks or dies slowly. And if he screams... we gag 'em and turn on the radio. Nobody gets an earful of nothin'."

"Okay, we go with that plan," Ricco said. "Understand, Mac?"

"Got it," Mac responded. The lobby door opened and closed.

"Let's move. Basement first." Ricco and Vinnie's footsteps headed for the cellar door.

Heart racing, Paul crouched under the stairs and surveyed his surroundings. Based on the sounds from above, he must be directly beneath the bustling restaurant. Most of the underground space was occupied by piles of crates, boxes, and furniture, along with various other supplies. A lone light bulb in the center of the ceiling cast a harsh glow over everything. Across the room, Paul spotted stairs he guessed went to the kitchen. Another set of steps, likely leading outside, was on the right wall. If he could just reach them...

He began to get up but froze when a soft shuffle of shoes on concrete came from the staircase. Heavy breathing and deliberate steps broke the silence as the two men cautiously advanced, each step a hunter's tread.

Paul crouched lower, surrounded by boxes of foodstuffs he hoped would be enough to conceal his presence, and held his breath. To avoid Ricco and Vinnie, he needed to stay quiet and motionless. Above all, he had to discover what happened to Dan.

***

Panic surged through Dan as he slipped off the ledge and started the plunge through the air. With one desperate lunge, which his body seemed to make with no direct input from his brain, he caught the edge of the granite lip with nothing more than the tips of his fingers. They cramped painfully as they gripped against the cold stone while he hung precariously in midair, like laundry left out to dry, four stories above the hard pavement below. Dan swallowed and worked to get his breathing more under control.

The unmistakable sounds of a commotion spilled out from the office—angry shouts and questions of the men inside echoing off the walls, chairs abruptly being pushed back from the desks, doors flung open with force.

"That's him!" Ricco's voice came from the hallway. "He must have slipped through the window!"

"Get him!" Vinnie yelled. "He may know too much!"

Heavy footsteps thudded down the corridor. Dan realized Vinnie must have caught sight of Paul and mistaken him for the figure that had been peering through the glass.

Dan's fingers began shaking from the strain as he clung to the ledge. His hands ached from trying to keep a hold, and his grip was becoming more precarious by the second. The fire escape, only two feet away, looked as far as two hundred miles.

"Come on, Dan," he told himself. "You can do this." He stared at his left hand and commanded it like a dog. "You. Move."

Dan summoned every ounce of energy and willpower. He wriggled his hand down the granite edge until he could reach no farther. Each movement sent jolts of pain shooting through his fingers, radiating down his arms. He refused to break his grip, no matter how much agony he felt.

"Your turn. Get going," he ordered his right hand.

His fingers shook as they inched along, finally meeting his other hand.

"Almost there," he said through gritted teeth. His muscles quivering, he stretched out his left hand until it gripped the metal of a banister. The right followed.

Sweat dripped down his face as he finally grasped the rails. He had made it—nothing else mattered. The soles of his shoes skimmed the railing of the platform below.

Dan pumped his legs like he was on a swing and released the rail when he was going forward. His body landed on the third-floor fire escape with a bone-crunching thud. He lay on the metal grating, exhausted, gasping. His hands had curled into claws. He let out a painful groan as he forced each finger straight.

"Got to find out about Paul," he panted, forcing himself back to his feet. "Can't leave him to face those goons alone."

Dan considered following the ladder to the ground and running to the restaurant for help. But that would involve the police asking awkward questions about why the brothers were sneaking around the building at night. Not to mention possibly putting Paul in danger if the thugs had already gotten their hands on him.

Time was not on his side. He decided to return to the fourth floor instead.

As he reached it, the door to the office swung open, and its light switched off. Dan ducked under the window as the door clicked shut.

Peeking over the sill, Dan glimpsed a short, pudgy man with stubby fingers walking down the dark corridor. Dan squinted as he leaned in to make out any defining features, but it was hopeless. One fact was certain, though: this was the big boss who sat in the desk chair. He was head of the protection racket. The man entered the elevator and vanished from sight.

****

Paul's heart raced as he pressed himself against the wall behind a stack of cardboard boxes. Ricco and Vinnie paused on the bottom step.

"Check that door," Vinnie whispered, pointing to one on the wall. "It could lead outside."

Ricco walked over, tried the handle, and returned to Vinnie. "No dice. He didn't get out that way."

"Now those stairs over there."

Ricco ran up the steps on the far side of the room and then came back to Vinnie. "Door at the top. Also locked."

"Right. He could be behind one of the boxes. We'll just have to flush him out," Ricco said. They split, each one moving along an aisle.

Paul slipped on his glasses as he searched for a way to escape, his gaze darting around the cramped basement. His eyes stopped on an open carton on the floor. He reached in and retrieved a can of peas. He weighed the tin in his hand, measuring the heaviness before looking at the single light bulb in the ceiling. Just then, the elevator started up, the machinery flooding the air with noise.

With one swift motion, Paul stood and threw the can with all his might. It connected precisely and shattered the bulb, plunging the room into darkness.

Ricco and Vinnie swore. Paul sprinted up the stairs, using the sound of the elevator to mask his footsteps, and closed the door behind him, shutting the two goons in pitch blackness.

"Jumpy insurance salesman with a gun," Paul said to himself as he pointed to the lobby door. "Dan went up to the fifth floor. Me, too."

Taking two stairs at a time, Paul dashed up to the top story, stepping into the darkened corridor. It was empty.

***

Dan cursed under his breath as he saw the plump spider scurry into the elevator and disappear. He climbed through the window, determined to find Paul. Reaching the office door, he hesitated. It was shut, but he couldn't be sure if it was locked. Despite his doubts, he knew he had to search inside for any clues.

"Wish me luck," he said to himself before turning the handle. The door opened, and he jogged to the inner office. He rummaged through every drawer and file cabinet, yet found nothing other than vacant chairs and an untouched desk. This place was likely only used for meetings.

His eyes fell on a telephone resting on the desktop. He picked it up and listened. No dial tone.

"Disconnected." He slammed the receiver down. "Of course it is."

He stepped back into the hall, wondering what had happened to Paul. He sprinted to the stairs, opened the door, and listened intently. Men's voices echoed up the stairwell from below. It sounded as if those goons hadn't caught Paul yet, but they had certainly managed to trap Dan inside the building. Time to escape using the fire escape.

He hurried back to the window and climbed onto the metal platform. He was about to start down toward the ground when the insurance salesman rounded the corner, stopping to light a cigarette. No exit that way. Hugging the bricks, Dan started up the ladder to the fifth floor.

***

"Dan? Dan?" Paul whispered. The darkness in the corridor swallowed the sound. He grumbled under his breath. "Where is my stupid brother?" He saw the open window, jogged to it, and listened. Somebody was climbing up the fire escape furtively, as though trying not to be detected. Paul pressed himself against the wall.

A figure emerged through the opening. Paul grabbed the person's arms and yanked him inside, both tumbling to the carpet. Paul pulled his arm back, ready to punch.

"Hey, careful!" Dan said, struggling to a seated position.

"Sorry." Relief flooded Paul at the sight of his twin. "I thought you were one of those dumb lugs."

"Help me shut this. Don't make any noise," Dan ordered.

Each brother took a side, easing the window closed. They sat on the floor.

"Why do that?" Paul gestured toward the glass.

"Because our friend, Mr. Gaudy Ring, is standing at the bottom of the fire escape," Dan answered. "And I don't think he wants to sell us a policy."

"Probably not. He's armed."

They were quiet for a moment.

"Now I catch what they're doing." Paul turned to Dan.

"What?"

"This building has three ways out. The stairs, the elevator and the fire escape." Paul held up three fingers on his right hand. "The same number of them. I'll bet each one will be covering one exit. Our problem: finding a fourth way out of here."

Dan spoke after a pause. "We could try the roof. The fire escape reaches it."

"Are you kidding?" Paul shot back, his brown eyes wide with disbelief. "Even if we could avoid the street watchdog, we'd still be trapped."

"Paul, we're boxed in no matter where we go." Desperation crept into Dan's voice. "At least they won't expect us to head up higher."

The idea of Vinnie and Ricco trapping them on the rooftop sent a chill down Paul. "Yeah, and they won't expect us to jump off the roof either, because that's the only thing we could do if they caught us up there."

"Okay, let's try the fire escape, anyway. We'll head down to the street," Dan said.

"Are you forgetting the insurance salesman down on the street, dope?" Paul shot back. "He's got a gun. We'd be like targets in a shooting gallery on that thing. Three shots for a quarter."

"Maybe he doesn't have good aim."

"Do you want to stop a bullet to find out?" Paul demanded.

"No," Dan glumly said. "Hey, what about the old-fashioned way? Let's stick our heads out the window and holler for help."

"That would give us away. Those goons could make it up here, take care of us, and still get away before the cops arrived. Maybe help us go all the way through the window," Paul said.

Dan sighed. "Yeah. We should hunker down here, I guess. Wait until a secretary shows up in the morning. Safety in numbers, and all that."

The elevator's shrieking whine knifed down the dark corridor, causing both of them to jump as they exchanged wary glances. After a short time, the noise died out into a deafening silence.

"The elevator was in the lobby." Dan glanced at the indicator: it was pointing at '2.' "Maybe somebody else has come to work late—"

Paul shook his head. His voice wavered as he spoke. "It's a squeeze play. The insurance salesman is by the fire escape. Either Ricco or Vinnie are in the elevator, while the other is climbing stairs. They must be searching this place floor by floor, bottom to top, office to office. We're the meat in the middle of a sandwich."

"Then we need someplace to hide," Dan said.

Paul searched the hallway for cover but found only plain walls. "Where? This corridor is bare... not even a potted palm."

Dan stood. "Let's try the doors. One might be unlocked because it's vacant or somebody forgot or didn't close it all the way. We find one open, get inside, and lock ourselves in. Then use the phone to call the cops."

Paul also got to his feet. "It's worth a go."

The two hustled down the hallway, trying every doorknob they passed. With every locked door they found, Paul grew more frantic, the surrounding air thickening with desperation. They moved like crazed night watchmen, seeking any room where they could hide.

The brothers ended up by the elevator. They looked at each other and shook their heads in defeat.

"Why don't we break into one?" Dan said. "Smash the glass and—"

"Why not hang a neon sign outside flashing 'they're hiding in here' while you're at it?" David shot back.

The elevator rumbled to life, shaking the walls of the narrow hallway and sucking Paul's breath away. The twin's eyes were glued to the indicator as is spun counter-clockwise, climbing relentlessly upward, marking off each floor like an ominous countdown to their fate.

It stopped.

"They're searching the third floor," Paul said.

Suddenly, Dan pointed down the hall. "Look! There's an open transom!"

Both ran to a door with a tantalizingly open window above it.

"There's not much room..." Paul started.

"Shut up and give me a boost! Just like before!" Dan said.

Paul locked his fingers together to form a makeshift step. With a nod to show he was ready, Dan planted his foot into Paul's palms and used his shoulder for leverage. Paul grunted as he thrust Dan off the ground as quickly as possible. Dan grabbed onto the bottom of the transom frame with both hands. He pulled himself up, attempting to wedge his body through the narrow opening. He didn't fit.

"Push me up higher," Dan said.

"I'm trying," Paul said with a groan as he hoisted his brother up.

The elevator whined up to the fourth floor.

"We're next! Move it!" Paul hissed.

Dan threw his arms over the sash and tried again to pull himself through the slot. "It's no good. Some holders stop the window opening wider."

"Well, yank the damn things out!"

Dan yanked at the stubborn brass catches. "No soap! They're screwed in! Let me down."

Paul's muscles trembled with fatigue as he lowered his brother to the floor. The elevator started again and continued its slow ascent. His head snapped toward the indicator, nearing the "5".

"They've got us cornered, buddy," he said.

Chapter Thirteen

Paul's heart pounded in sync with the faint hum of the elevator ascending toward the fifth floor. His mind raced, broad strokes forming an image like one of Dan's pencil sketches. The picture became clear when he realized that Ricco, Vinnie, and Mac had made a crucial mistake—they thought there was only one "kid", not two.

"Dan, they don't know we're twins, that we're a pair. They haven't seen us together. We'll use that to our advantage. Hold the stairwell door closed and keep whoever it is out," Paul whispered, his voice barely audible over the whirring gears in the elevator shaft. "I'll handle this guy first."

Dan nodded and approached the door. His muscles tensed as he wrapped his hand around the doorknob and pulled his lanky body against it. Bracing his feet on the frame, he put all of his weight into holding it shut.

Paul moved toward the elevator and flattened himself along the wall, tense and rigid, the vibrations of the machinery rumbling through his shirt. A film of sweat appeared on his forehead as he clenched his fists tight.

The indicator stopped at '5' and dinged, announcing the arrival to their floor. The outer metal door slid open with a low groan, followed by the rattling of the interior cage door. Vinnie stepped out cautiously. His gaze immediately locked onto Dan, and a twisted grin spread across his face.

"Ricco! Get up here! I found him!" Vinnie shouted toward the stairwell. He started for Dan. "Thought you could outsmarts us, huh punk?"

"Why, the thought never occurred to us." Dan flashed an innocent smile.

Vinnie looked confused. "Huh... what... us?"

Paul reached out and grabbed Vinnie's shoulder to spin him around. "Yeah, us." As soon as their eyes met, Paul threw all his strength into a single right cross that crashed into hood's jaw with such force that it sent him spiraling to the ground, out cold.

"Ding! That round goes to you," Dan said as he hung onto the door.

"Thanks," Paul replied. "Round two coming up."

"Hey, Vinnie! What's goin' on?" Ricco's voice echoed from the stairwell. The door thumped as he tried to wrench it open.

Dan gritted his teeth as he pulled against the door, battling Ricco's forceful tugs from the stairwell. "Hurry, please."

"Ready?" Paul asked, taking a position opposite the door with a determined expression on his face.

"Ready." Dan grimaced under the strain of holding the door closed.

Paul braced himself. "Okay, on three. One... two... THREE!"

When Ricco pulled back, Dan released the door and quietly moved out of view. Ricco tumbled backward into the stairwell wall, rage etched across his face.

Paul smiled and waved. "Hi there, big boy!"

Ricco let loose a bellow and rushed for Paul. When he crossed the threshold, Dan stuck his leg out, tripping Ricco mid-charge. The goon stumbled forward, off balance, right into Paul's embrace.

"Please! We hardly know each other!" Paul said.

Dan grabbed Ricco's arms and pulled them behind his back. Paul delivered a solid one-two punch to Ricco's chin, followed by an uppercut. Ricco's eyes rolled back, and Dan let him slump to the floor.

"Thank you for your assistance, my dear brother," Paul said to Dan as he brushed off his hands, "but that really wasn't very sporting of you."

Dan shrugged. "So sue me." Vinnie groaned and stirred. "I think it's time we scrammed out of this clambake."

"Yeah, it was getting boring anyway," Paul said. "Come on, let's beat it!"

Paul grabbed Dan's arm and guided him to the door. They raced down the stairs, their hurried footsteps echoing through the empty stairwell. They stopped when they reached the lobby.

"Walk out calm, cool, and collected," Dan said. "We don't want a passerby calling the cops on us for an assault and battery charge."

Paul nodded, took a deep breath, and unlocked the deadbolt knob on the glass doors. The brothers walked out into the evening and headed for their jeep. While they crossed the street, Paul glanced back at the building and spotted Mac standing on the corner. They locked gazes for a second before Paul tore his eyes away.

"Don't look now," Paul said, "but Mr. Gaudy Ring is across the street, keeping an eye on us."

"Yeah, I saw him, but we can't worry about that now. Let's get out of here first," Dan said. "Pick up the pace."

Paul nodded, and the two walked faster. They reached the jeep.

Paul climbed into the driver's seat while Dan clambered into the passenger side. Paul revved the engine and sped off down the street. As they waited for the stop light a few blocks away, the twins looked at each other and laughed.

Paul steered onto the highway, heading towards Farmingford, the headlights cutting through the night. The washed-out trees raced by, interrupted by a faint glow from a farmhouse window in the distance. The twins remained quiet; they had learned that talking was difficult with the jeep's noisy four-cylinder motor roaring and gusts of wind creating a deafening noise inside the open cab.

Dan glanced behind him, then leaned over and yelled into his brother's ear. "Hey, Paul, how fast are we going?"

"As fast as we can in this thing... 45," Paul called back. "Why?"

"A car has been following us since we left town. It hasn't passed yet. Most do on the highway." Dan looked over his shoulder again. "I think we're being followed."

"By who?" Paul checked the rearview mirror.

"By whom. A dark sedan, I think. Maybe our friends from the office." Dan continued to watch the mysterious vehicle. "We can't lead them back to our house. We need a plan."

"I'll turn onto 364. If they follow, we'll know for sure." Paul suggested.

"Right."

"Let's see if our tail likes surprises." Paul swerved onto Highway 364. They navigated the lonely rural road, their lights illuminating the pavement ahead. Paul held his breath, waiting to see if the black sedan would follow.

"They're still behind us," Dan yelled.

Paul wondered if he had made a mistake. There was nothing at all on this route, not even a gas station, for another twenty miles.

The black sedan's headlights loomed ominously in the rearview mirror, and cast monstrous shadows across the highway. Paul kept the accelerator pedal pressed to the floor, trying to keep some distance between them and their followers.

The sedan's engine roared as it barreled forward. It swerved dangerously close to the edge of the road, the scent of burning rubber filling the air. Like a predatory cheetah pursuing its prey, it gained on the jeep until its front fender was mere inches away from colliding with the rear fender. With a jolt, the sedan cut in and violently bumped the jeep, causing Paul to fight for control as the vehicles raced down the road. But just as quickly as it had advanced, the car dropped back. It moved out of the lane to try again.

"They're trying to run us into the ditch!" Dan shouted.

Paul jerked the jeep to straddle the double yellow line, cutting off the black sedan. "Now let them try it!"

The sedan again charged towards them, aiming directly for the passenger side of the jeep. Paul's grasp on the steering wheel tightened as he calculated his next move. In a split-second decision, he jerked the wheel to the right, causing the car following to swerve and narrowly miss their vehicle. The screech of tires fills the air as Paul expertly blocked the car from overtaking them again.

"Keep them busy!" Dan yelled.

Paul's knuckles turned white as he gripped the steering wheel, his foot heavy on the gas as he pushed the jeep to its limits down the empty highway. He careened left and right, his heart racing with adrenaline as he tried to outmaneuver the sedan that pursued them. The two vehicles engaged in a wild dance, their tires screaming in protest as they battled and swerved on the open road. Paul's eyes locked on the rearview mirror as the wolf-like sedan nipped at their heels.

Dan clambered over the front seat, grappling for balance as the jeep swung wildly back and forth across the highway. He waited until the sedan pulled up behind them, its headlights blinding him. In one swift movement, he grabbed the toolbox and hurled it with all his might at the car. "Bombs away!"

The toolbox smashed into the hood, leaving a noticeable dent before bouncing and striking the windshield. The sedan's driver slammed on the brakes, causing the toolbox to fly off and soar through the air. The wheels locked up, and thick black smoke poured out from the brakes, screeching against the pavement as the car spun in a full circle.

"Direct hit!" Dan leaned over the front seat and yelled into Paul's ear, "Try the old highway."

"Why?" Dan asked, puzzled.

"They abandoned the loop when they built the new bridge—"

"And the old bridge is out!" Paul gave a wicked grin. "I bet they don't know that."

"Let's give 'em a tour, buddy!" Dan patted one hand on Paul's shoulder.

His brother made a hard turn onto the old highway, the jeep's tires wailing in protest and Dan clinging to the seat to keep from being thrown out at the sudden change in direction. The jeep lurched and rattled over the rough and potholed pavement. Paul slowed as they approached the switchback that wrapped around the hill.

"Over there!" Dan pointed to a clump of bushes large enough to conceal their jeep.

Paul veered off the road, slid the vehicle behind the thicket, and cut the engine and lights.

"Let's go!" Dan started to sprint up the slope before he had finished speaking. His twin was right on his heels. They leaped over fallen logs and scrambled up the steep incline through the trees, their feet sending a trail of dirt and leaves into the air with each step. On the way up, they heard the squeal of tires. Paul checked in back of him as a pair of headlights swung onto the road.

"Here they come," he jerked his thumb toward the highway. "They took the bait."

"They'll have to slow down because of the condition of the pavement," Dan said.

Cresting the top of the hill, they careened down the other side, having trouble keeping their footing as they slid on the loose soil. When they reached the road, they skidded to an abrupt stop, taking just a few seconds to fill their lungs.

"There it is," Paul panted, pointing at the temporary "Bridge Out" barricade sitting on the asphalt.

They raced down the pavement, reaching the barricade at top speed. The two lined up by the sign, each grabbing an end tightly.

"People really shouldn't leave things in the middle of the street," Paul said.

"Very inconsiderate."

The two groaned as they lifted the barrier, slowly moving it behind some bushes.

"Quick, down!" Dan motioned as the sound of an approaching motor reached their ears. They crouched in the underbrush.

"Think they'll fall for it?" Paul asked, trying to keep his voice steady. "I mean, this is right out of a cartoon."

"Let's just hope so," Dan replied, crossing his fingers.

The black sedan's engine roared as it came into sight, turning the bend in the distance, tires screeching as it struggled to maintain control around the corner. It accelerated when it reached the straight section of the road.

"Zoom, zoom, zoom." Dan's breath was hitched in anticipation. "Faster! Faster!"

The sedan's headlamps cut through the night as it sped past the brother's hiding spot. A few seconds later, the driver desperately tried to stop the car. Its wheels locked up and threw up a spray of dirt, pieces of gravel flying off the wheels like bullets.

But it was too late for the brakes to do any good. The taillights glowed red through the thin layer of dust thrown in the air before everything went dark. There was a thunderous crash followed by an awful crunching and splash as the car hurtled off the downed bridge, plummeting into the murky mud below.

Dan and Paul stood and ran forward, their eyes peering over the concrete wall that marked the abutment. At first, all they picked up in the dark was the sound of gurgling water. However, a patch of light glimmered from about five hundred feet away.

The sedan was stuck in the streambed. It was right-side up but tilted at a strange angle, with water flowing over its tire rims. The one headlight still functioning shone upwards towards the stars. A figure moved around the left front wheel before standing up and speaking his words in the still night air.

"The mud is so deep it could sink a battleship!" The voice was filled with anger. It was Vinnie. "We're going to have to get a wrecker in here!" He stomped back along the side of the car, creating loud, splashing sounds.

The reply roared back from Ricco. "Then go call one, you idiot!"

"Why don't you do it yourself!" Vinnie growled back. "It was your idea to go down this cow track after them!"

"This is where they turned! I seen it!" Ricco protested.

A third voice cut in, probably Mac. "Quit arguing and figure out how we're going to get back to the boss and tell him what happened. He won't be happy."

"Oh, you always worry!" snapped Vinnie.

"Maybe we can pick up their trail again," Ricco said.

"Stop talking nonsense!" Vinnie shouted. "They must be miles from here already! All we can say is that the last time we saw them, they were traveling east. If I ever get my hands on those kids again..."

"One of us needs to go find a phone on the highway," Mac said. "Where?"

"There's a map in here someplace." Ricco sounded a little calmer. "Check it to see if there's a town somewhere close by."

One of the men slogged through the murky water to a window. A yellow flashlight beam illuminated the car's interior while he squinted to look.

"It worked!" Paul exclaimed.

"Keep quiet," Dan cautioned, though he couldn't suppress a grin. "Come on. Mom taught us to return things to their proper place. Let's put that barricade back and get out of here."

Together, they heaved the sign back into place. They jogged back to their jeep, barely able to hold their laughter in until they were in their seats.

"Nice work, my young brother," Paul clapped Dan on the shoulder as they climbed back into their seats.

"I'm younger by only two minutes, remember?" Dan stressed, holding up two fingers.

"Still counts." Laughing, Paul started up the jeep and drove home. The downstairs lights were on when they pulled into the driveway. "Mom's still up."

Dan nodded as climbed out of the jeep and opened the back door. He looked down at Paul's hands as they walked through the kitchen. "Knuckles," he warned out of the corner of his mouth. Paul put his hands in his pockets, hiding his bruised knuckles.

They stepped into the living room. Mrs. Case was listening to the radio, an open magazine in her lap. "How was the movie?" she asked.

"It was good," Paul responded. Dan nodded.

"What did you see?" Mrs. Case put her reading to one side, giving her attention to her sons.

After a moment's pause, the twins answered at once.

"*A Matter of Life and Death*," Paul said.

"*The Chase*," Dan said.

Mrs. Case cast a questioning glance at the boys.

"It was a double feature," Dan clarified.

"What was your favorite part?" she asked.

"Gee, there were lots. It's kind of hard to pick one." Paul turned to his brother. "What was yours, Dan?"

Dan shot Paul a dirty look. "Ah... I think it was when the henchmen chased the heroes around that office building."

"Oh, yeah! Pow! Pow!" Paul threw some punches in the air, before quickly putting his hands behind his back. "Remember the car chase? When the good guys tricked the bad guys into driving off a downed bridge?"

Dan joined Paul's laughter. "Yeah, yeah, that was great, too." He used his hands to demonstrate, adding sound effects.

Mrs. Case smiled. "I'm glad you enjoyed yourselves."

"It certainly was an exciting night," Dan said. He yawned. "Well, I'm for hitting the sack. Night, Mom."

"Me, too," Paul agreed. "Night, Mom."

"Good night, boys. See you in the morning." Mrs. Case went back to her magazine.

The two brothers walked down the hall in silence. When they reached Paul's bedroom door, he paused and looked back at Dan, motioning towards his room. Dan nodded and Paul opened his door, flicking on the lights. He pretended to get ready for bed, shuffling items in his dresser before turning off the lights. Minutes later, Dan's face appeared at the window and Paul silently opened it for him.

"I'm to be going in and out of windows a lot tonight," Dan said as he climbed in. They both sat down on Paul's bed, speaking in hushed tones to avoid being heard.

"Well, what happened to you? On the fire escape?" Paul asked.

"I couldn't see anything, so I shimmied out on the ledge..." Dan started.

"You did what!" Paul stood.

"Shh! Don't talk so loud! Do want Mom to hear you?" Dan hissed. "Yeah, I decided to get the perspective of a pigeon. I peeked in through the window."

"What did you find out?"

Dan shrugged. "Nothing much, unfortunately. The boss was there, paying off Vinnie, Ricco, and the insurance guy…"

"Mac. I think his name is Mac."

"Okay, Mac," Dan said. "Then Vinnie spotted me, and that kicked off all the fun."

"Did you get a load of the head guy? Who was he? What did he look like?"

"Ahh, it's the same thing as with the rest of this whole business." Dan threw up his hands. "He sat at the desk, facing away from the window, so the tall back of the chair hid him. After everybody took off to chase you, I saw him walk down the hall. The dark corridor with no lights. With his back to me," he stressed. "All I can say is that he is short and pudgy. I got into the office and checked it. Nothing. Completely empty. They must have used it only for meetings."

The two sat in disappointed silence for a minute.

"Well, at least we have Ricco's last name," Paul said. "That's something we can pass that to Detective Barton."

"I don't know what good that would do." Dan leaned forward on his knees and stared into the carpet. "He could run a background check, sure, but he'd have to throw out a dragnet to catch him. That would be certain to warn the protection racket that the cops are on to them. They'd assume one of their 'clients' snitched. That could trigger retributions against all of them."

"The restaurant? The office? What about them?" Paul pressed.

"You can bet Ricco and Vinnie won't be eating at La Dolce Vita any time soon. Ditto using 'Murdstone Inc.' again." Dan flopped back on the bed. "I'm afraid, my dear brother, we've hit a dead end."

Chapter Fourteen

The bell above the drugstore door jingled, announcing Paul's entrance. He glanced at the rows of candy, trying to decide between two different bars, when he spotted Betty and Donna finishing their root beer floats as they sat at the soda fountain. His brother was working behind the counter, his hands a blur as he created two banana splits, humming a tune under his breath. He delivered the treats to a couple at a small table, then returned to the counter.

"How are the two prettiest little lasses in this part of the county enjoin' their refreshments?" Dan said in the voice of a movie cowboy.

Donna gave him a devilish smile, and played her role, twisting a strand of her hair around a finger. "Why, they're mighty fine, sir. Tell me, are all the cowboys in this neck of the woods as good-lookin' as you?"

"Aw, shucks." Dan looked at the floor and pretended to kick a rock with one foot. He noticed Paul and then nodded to one of the small tables. "Ma'am, can I show you the north forty?"

"Why, sure 'nough, pa'dner." Donna picked up her float, and the two moved away from the counter.

Paul took a deep breath and edged closer to the fountain. He cleared his throat and tried to sound casual. "Uh, hi, Betty. Mind if I sit here?"

Betty shrugged. "Of course. It's a free country."

Paul slid onto the chrome stool next to hers. Dan returned behind the counter, drew a soda, and placed it in front of his twin. Paul reached into his pocket. Dan waved him off. "Here you go, your usual. On the house."

"Thanks, buddy. It helps to have friends in high places." He grinned and took a sip, savoring the cold sweetness hitting his tongue like a wave of relief.

Dan went back to Donna. Paul and Betty sat in an awkward silence for a minute.

Betty finally spoke, "How's everything been?"

"Fine," Paul replied. "How about you?"

"Fine. I've been busy with school and cheerleading practice and stuff."

They fell quiet again.

"Yeah, just thought I'd swing by and pick up a snack. I didn't know you were here," he said. Another strained pause. "And, um, I miss you."

"I miss you too," she said softly.

The two sipped their drinks.

"Listen, Betty," Paul ventured cautiously, "why can't we just eat lunch at school together? It's not like a date or anything."

"You know why. My father doesn't want me to see you." Her voice had an edge he hadn't heard before. She finished the last spoonful of ice cream out of the glass.

Paul's heart sank. "At all?"

"You and my dad had a 'disagreement'—that's what you called it." Betty used her straw to stir the bottom of her empty root beer float glass. "Neither one of you will tell me why or what it's about. I'm on the outside, looking in."

"Betty, I told you. I can't—" Paul started.

"I know, I know, you can't tell me. It's part of some deep, dark secret," Betty said.

"It's true," Paul insisted.

"He doesn't want me to see you," Betty said firmly.

"But—"

"Did you do what your father asked of you when he was alive?" Betty challenged.

Paul bristled. Betty was swinging low. She knew how much he respected his dad. "Yes, of course I did."

"The same here. My dad's not happy about us being together right now. He wants me to stop. So I will." Betty said.

"I understand." Paul slumped over his soda.

"If you and he worked things out—" Betty said.

Paul rubbed his hands over his face as though he was bone tired. He hinted to Mr. Wilson that he knew he was the target of the protection racket, suggesting the store owner speak up to the police without fear. Then Paul remembered he didn't have a business, wife, or daughter to worry about, unlike Mr. Wilson.

Could he ask someone else to risk everything, even if it was for the right thing?

And as his brother had said, they had reached a dead end. All the two held were bits and pieces of information. Perhaps useful to Detective Barton, perhaps not. So there they were, stuck in neutral. Pressing harder on the accelerator wouldn't help, and possibly could make things worse.

"I can't," Paul said at last, staring at the marble counter.

"I'm sorry then." Betty stood. "Are you ready, Donna? We really need to hotfoot it."

Paul cradled his head in one hand and pushed his glass around in small circles. Donna and Dan rose from the table where they were seated.

"Ready, Betty." She turned to Dan and smiled. "You make great root beer floats, handsome. And the company's not too bad, either."

Dan grinned. "Thanks."

After the girls left, Dan collected their glasses and dumped them in the tub with the other dirty dishes. He pulled out a towel and started to wipe down the counter, stopping when he reached his brother.

"Don't ask." Paul kept his eyes on his drink.

"Okay, okay, I won't." Dan gestured toward the glass. "Do you want another?"

Paul shook his head. Dan continued working his way down the fountain.

"Oh, remember tonight Mom is having dinner and playing bridge at the Holts. I think they're still trying to play matchmaker," Dan said. "I'll wait until Ted comes on and eat here. Free food. One perk of this job. Do you want to use the jeep to get something?"

Paul sighed and nodded. He sat up, drained the rest of his drink in one gulp, and handed the empty to Dan. "Thanks for the soda."

"You bet." Dan put the glass with the other dirty ones. He showed a direction with a jerk of his head. "The jeep is around the corner."

Paul grunted a response and got up. An elderly couple entered the drugstore and took seats at a table. With a wave to Paul, Dan grabbed a pair of menus and hustled over to the new customers, greeting them cheerfully.

Paul's feet dragged as he approached the jeep, torn between going for a burger or heading home. He enjoyed seeing the guys from school at the drive-in but didn't want to talk to them now, not the way he felt. So he drove to his house instead.

When he entered the living room, his gaze was drawn towards the mantle above the fireplace. A framed photograph of his father in his army uniform smiled out from its frame. Next to it was a small, rectangular banner with a blue border and gold star, the symbol for being killed in action.

Betty had been right. She knew he wouldn't defy his dad by not doing what he asked, so he couldn't blame Betty, either.

Paul went into the kitchen and took out a can of pork and beans from the cupboard. He opened it with a sigh, dumping the contents into a pot on the stove with a loud sploosh.

"Yummy," he mumbled to himself as he heated his supper in the saucepan, then slopped it into a bowl. He grabbed a spoon and ate with no enthusiasm. When he finished, he washed his dish and wiped it dry. The phone rang, startling him. Paul ran the towel over his hands and flung it over his shoulder before picking up the receiver.

"Case residence," he answered.

"You think it's ended, pal?" a voice said. "It hasn't."

"What hasn't? Who is this?"

"I wonder what pretty boy can do outside the ring," came the taunt over the wire.

"Jake? Is that you?" Paul asked.

"Who else, smart guy?" Jake fired back. "Well?"

"Well, what?"

"Don't be such a dope," Jake sneered. "We need to finish what we started at the YMCA. This time somewhere nobody can stop us."

"Jake, I don't want to—"

Jake interrupted with a derisive snort. "Yellow, huh? I thought so. You're not such a big tough guy if you can't wear gloves and have Bud there to help you out. You're just plain gutless."

Paul took a deep breath to control his temper. "Jake, I'm not a coward..."

"No? Could have fooled me. You're sure acting like a yellow belly." The words were aimed with the sureness of rifle shots.

It took a lot of effort for Paul to keep his voice calm. "Jake, we need to talk—"

"Boy, wait until I spread it around to the guys at the YMCA." Jake clucked like a chicken.

"All right, where? Name the place, name the time, pal," Paul exploded into the phone. "I'm going to shove what you said back down your throat."

"Bronsell Park, in one hour," Jake shot back. "I'll be waiting for you to show up... but I'm not holding my breath."

The line went dead, leaving Paul to sputter angrily at the dial tone. He slammed down the receiver. As he turned, he caught the eyes of his father's photo. "I'm sorry, Dad. I have to do this."

***

Bonsell Park, sandwiched with a cornfield on one side and a vast pasture on the other, was located off a two-lane highway between Farmingford and Belmont. Despite its unimpressive appearance, the park offered the necessary amenities: a baseball diamond, picnic tables, and a playground. With the baseball field lights off, the park was cloaked in a bleak darkness apart from a few scattered lampposts that threw dim yellow halos across the ground.

As Paul pulled into the lot, it was clear he was the only one there. Parking the jeep, he stepped out, his pulse beating in his ears. He made his way to the center of the park and paused. A metallic squeaking noise coming from the nearby swing set broke the quiet. Paul turned towards the sound.

He squinted through the poor light, trying to see who was sitting in one of the seats. The figure's feet rested on the ground, rocking on the swing with occasional chain squeals from above.

"You have more guts than I thought." Jake hopped off the seat and swaggered to Paul.

"Jake, we don't have to go through with this," Paul said. "It's done. It's over. You tried to beat up my brother. I paid you back. It may have been wrong of me to do that, but I was mad. We can work this out—"

"Yeah? By you and what army?" Jake mocked.

"I don't want to fight you, Jake."

"No? Then your face is going to look like a mess when I'm finished with it, pal. It's up to you. Time to see what you're made of, pretty boy." Jake took off his shirt and tossed it on a picnic table.

Paul stood there. He didn't know what to do. His pride warred with his fear, both battling for dominance in his mind. He didn't want to be beaten up without putting up a fight. Yet, he understood that if he backed out, he would always be branded as a coward by the guys. Not to mention it would teach Jake that fists were the only means of settling things. But sometimes, however, they were...

He pulled off his shirt and dropped it to the ground, his muscles already tense. Planting his feet on the grass, he took a deep breath and got himself into the guard position. This was it.

The two squared off, the air electric with tension. Jake struck first like a rattlesnake, his fists flying in a blur of motion. Paul blocked most of the jabs with his forearms, but one made contact with his jaw, sending a shockwave through his body and his head snapping back. He stumbled back, adrenaline rushing through him as he prepared to continue the bout.

The fighters shifted their stances and exchanged another flurry of punches, blocking the other's attacks with impressive skill. Both boys eyed his opponent warily as they circled each other, seeking an opening for an attack.

Paul unleashed a storm of blows. Jake ducked and weaved with lightning speed, every punch meeting its perfect counter. Paul's left jab struck like a cobra, followed by an unstoppable hook. The sweat dripping from their bodies glistened in the dim light of the lamps like diamond dust, their chests heaving as they struggled to catch their breath. It was like a ballet of fury, a dizzying and deadly display of power and skill.

Jake threw a shot toward Paul's gut. Paul tightened his abdominal muscles in preparation, but the blow lacked power. He realized Jake hadn't been hitting with the full force he knew from experience he was capable of. Jake was pulling his punches. There was a hesitation in his movements, too. It appeared Jake didn't want to fight, but perhaps only put on a show. But who was the audience?

They went into a clinch. Paul tried to break free of Jake, but he was held tight.

"Consolidated Paint Company. Tonight," Jake whispered in Paul's ear. "Now take a dive and stay down."

The two boxers released their clinch, each taking a few steps back. Jake cocked his arm and threw a right cross that barely grazed

Paul's chin. Paul stumbled backward, arms flailing to maintain balance before collapsing into the dirt. He lay still, eyes closed.

"There, pretty boy," Jake snarled while catching his breath. "Now we're even Stephen."

Paul stayed on the ground as Jake ran away and a vehicle drove up. In a minute, he heard another voice. Ricco's.

"Vinnie and I watched from across the highway," Ricco said. "Who is that other guy? I can't see him from here."

"He's a nobody. I was just settling a personal grudge," Jake answered.

"You sure took care of him!" Vinnie said approvingly.

"Yeah, I sure took care of him," Jake responded in a flat tone.

The sound of car doors opening and shutting reached Paul, followed a few moments later by the engine revving as it raced into the night. Once only crickets chirping broke the stillness, Paul opened his eyes and slowly sat up.

He pulled up his knees and wrapped his arms around them. Now he held no doubts. No maybes remained. Jake was in the gang. Ricco and Vinnie had convinced him to work for them after Paul had refused.

"Stupid guy," he said to himself without malice. His mind turned to his parents, and he couldn't help but wonder if it was what they went through at Jake's age. The promise of wealth, power and respect lured them into joining Lorenzo Rizzo's bootlegging gang in Chicago. They escaped that dangerous world. Could Jake do it, too?

Paul stood and picked up his shirt. Possibly the fake fight had a deeper meaning than both their egos. Was Jake trying to provoke Paul into a fight to escape the protection racket? By doing so, he was risking everything to send a message—to warn Paul about the upcoming target of the gang: Consolidated Paint Company. Was this his way of asking for help, or was it more sinister?

He threw on his shirt and ran to the park's public phone booth to look up the address of the Consolidated Paint Company, only to find the directory missing. Muttering a curse in frustration, he sprinted back to the jeep, jumping in and hitting the accelerator. The wheels of the jeep kicked up puffs of dust from the pavement as he drove home. He had something to do and needed his twin's help.

Pulling into the driveway, he saw lights in the workshop. He burst inside. Dan sat at his table, working on the drawing that was for the school yearbook title page.

"Have you got any film in your camera?" Paul demanded.

Dan put down his pencil. "Well, and a good evening to you, too."

"Is your camera loaded?" Paul almost yelled.

"No, but I've got some film," Dan answered, puzzled.

"Anything that would work in low light?"

"There's a roll of Super XX—" Dan gestured toward the dark-room.

"Load it and meet me at the jeep," Paul said.

"Wait... what... why? What's this all about?" Dan protested.

"Don't argue!" Paul snapped. "Do it!"

Dan got up and raised his hands in surrender. "Okay... alright... doing it."

Paul flew to the house and banged into the living room. He yanked open the drawer of the side table and grabbed the white, tattered phone directory. His finger slid down its columns of information until he spotted a small heading in bold: Consolidated Paint Company. The company was located just outside Belmont. He scribbled down its address on an old envelope. Stuffing the book back, he dashed to the jeep. Dan already sat in the passenger seat, camera slung around his neck.

"May I be so forward as to ask what's going on?" Dan asked as Paul backed out of the driveway. "I mean, before we go charging off somewhere like the Marines?"

Paul shifted the jeep into gear and accelerated down the street, heading for the highway. As he drove, he told Dan what had taken place at the park.

Dan leaned toward his brother to be heard over the engine. "So this Jake guy is working with Vinnie and Ricco?"

"It looks like it," Paul answered, rolling through the stop sign at the corner and pressing the gas. "They must have offered the enforcer job to him after I said no."

"Is he the one who punched me at the hardware store?"

"Seems likely." Paul grumbled, "We need to get a faster car."

"So he talked you into a fake fight to tell you about this paint place," Dan said. "You think it's the next target?"

Paul nodded as he stopped the jeep at Farmingford's sole traffic light.

"Then why not just call the cops?" Dan asked. "Catch those goons in the act?"

"Because I'm not totally sure Jake is telling the truth," Paul answered.

"You're not sure?" Dan said in disbelief. "Then why—"

"I think what he said is probably true, but I still don't trust him completely." Paul slammed his foot on the gas as the signal turned green. "If he works for Ricco and Vinnie, he could have told me the company name as a decoy. Suppose we have the police raid the paint company, but the gang fires a different building across town. Detective Barton would never believe us about anything else if that happened. It also may get us in trouble with the law. Filing a false police report and all that."

"If Jake is right about the location, what's our plan?" Dan grabbed the windshield as Paul took a sharp turn. "Yell 'come out with your hands up. We got you surrounded'?"

"No." Paul leaned toward his brother and grinned. "I thought about that night by the Davis warehouse. You didn't take any pictures then, but I'm hoping my talented twin brother will take some excellent and incriminating photos of Vinnie and Ricco in the act tonight."

Dan was quiet for a minute. "Of course, this whole thing could be something else."

"What?"

"A trap."

Chapter Fifteen

The Consolidated Paint Company had to be the ugliest building Dan had ever seen. Square and squat, it perched next to the railroad tracks outside Belmont. It boasted four dismal stories made of plain gray cement, a metal-roofed loading dock along the rails, and narrow, high windows precisely spaced throughout the walls. Dan thought a more appropriate name would be the "Consolidated Prison Company". Even the windowless brick warehouse next to it looked more elegant in comparison.

The two structures stood like castles, isolated from their surroundings. Weathered "For Sale Build to Suit" signs sprouted in the vacant lots around them, remnants of an industrial development halted by the war that never restarted. Some streetlights were installed, but had no globes; wires poked from the ends of the posts. Rectangles of weeds were surrounded precisely laid-out streets. Beyond the plots, farmland stretched as far as they could see. Civilization's presence was only suggested by faint glow of Belmont's lights in the distance.

Paul parked behind some bushes, and the brothers climbed out of their jeep. They surveyed the area, looking for any sign of movement or danger. All was still and quiet apart from the rustling of the cool night breeze through weeds as they walked toward the paint company along a wide road.

"No other car around," Dan said. "What did they do? Take a taxi here?"

Paul nodded at the warehouse. "It could be on the far side of that place. Or parked behind some bushes, like we are."

Dan grunted an affirmative response. He scanned the concrete building. "Nothing's up at the paint company."

"There's no activity that we can *see*, my dear brother," Paul corrected. "Let's just look first."

"Why not? We're out here," Dan shrugged.

Shadows draped the front part of the building. A half-glassed door marked "Entrance", with a window right next to it, were both covered by tightly closed blinds that blocked out any trace of light shining from inside. Paul reached out and twisted the doorknob. Locked. He gestured to Dan to go around the side.

They walked, stopping at a door halfway down the wall. The scattering of cigarette butts on the dirt showed that it was a popular spot for employees to take breaks. Dan tried the door, and it moved inward with a slight sound. He cautiously opened it up part-way and peered in. Dan pulled a pencil flashlight from his pocket and grinned at Paul.

"Came prepared this time," Dan whispered. He couldn't keep the triumph out of his voice. "Come on."

The two stepped inside and shut the door behind them, finding themselves in a dark, narrow hallway. Dan risked switching on his flash. It illuminated steps going up on their right, leading into the gloom of the floor above. In front of them was a door that opened to a small bathroom, with its walls, sink, and toilet were all painted an unappealing gray. The corridor angled away to their left, voices murmuring within earshot. Dan turned off his flashlight.

Hearts pounding, they crept to the end of the hall, peeking around the corner. About ten feet from them, a thick metal sliding door blocked the passageway, and a thin sliver of light shined from beneath it. Muffled sounds emanated from the far side.

Paul tapped his brother on the shoulder and pointed up. Dan nodded, and they retraced their steps to the stairs. With caution, Dan tested the first tread, only to realize the stairs were concrete, just like the rest of the building. Walking as softly as possible, the two climbed to the second story.

They stood in a forest of metal shelves, Dan's flash the only source of light. The narrow, endless rows held boxes and cans that stretched back into darkness. More stacks rested on pallets lining the walls. With Dan in the lead, they ventured deeper into the silent maze. The air was thick with the sweet scent of turpentine and linseed oil, making Dan's head spin slightly.

Paul sniffed, then put his lips next to Dan's ear. "That smells awfully strong, doesn't it? Even for a paint company."

Dan nodded in reply. The brothers followed their noses, the odor becoming so overwhelming Dan had to stifle a cough until they reached the center of the floor. They came face to face with a pile of stacked shipping pallets, soaked with paint thinner, the empty cans lying nearby.

Dan leaned into Paul and whispered. "Ricco and Vinnie are busy little beavers, aren't they?"

The door echoed below, followed by determined, precise footsteps in the hallway. The sliding door opened and closed.

Dan caught sight of a freight elevator. The box-like platform usually moved up and down, but now was stopped at a higher floor. Dim light seeped through the open shaft, only blocked by a chain across the gap. Dan grasped Paul's arm and pulled him towards it as voices floated up from below.

"We got everything set up, boss," Ricco was saying.

"Yeah, a surprise on every floor," Vinnie put in.

"Good. Make sure it's big. Send a message to those other suckers who think they can report us to the police," the boss said. "Arson's always an excellent way to show our product's benefits."

"We'll do our best, boss," Vinnie said, "but me and Ricco have been thinkin'."

"Thinking?" came the suspicious reply.

Dan held the flashlight out for Paul to take, then picked up his camera. While Paul showed the light, Dan twisted the knobs to the settings he wanted.

"Yeah. This here job is important. It's taken up a lot of our valuable time," Ricco said.

"What!" the boss snapped.

"So me and Ricco think we deserve more dough," Vinnie said.

After finishing the settings, Dan knelt on the concrete floor. "Hold my legs," he said to Paul in a quiet voice.

He adjusted his position until he was lying flat on the ground with his waist resting at the edge of the shaft. As Paul gripped Dan's ankles, he held the camera out in front of him.

The boss was going on. "This is hardly the time or place for such discussions."

"Vinnie and I figure it's as good a time as any," Ricco said.

Dan gritted his teeth and bent forward, suppressing a groan as he hung down. He still couldn't see out from the lower floor's elevator doorway. He waved one arm in Paul's direction, signaling him to drop him lower. With shuffling feet and quiet grunts, Paul hoisted Dan's ankles and let his brother down a little farther.

That was just enough. Dan peeked out the shaft opening, hanging upside down like a bat. Vinnie, Ricco, and a man—the same one Dan saw leaving the office—huddled by a lantern. Their argument continued in hushed, urgent tones.

"I mean, you don't want us spilling everything we know, do you?" Vinnie needled.

Dan held the camera up to his eye and snapped a photo as Vinnie spoke, his voice covering the sound of the shutter. Dan slowly and quietly advanced the film.

"Are you trying to blackmail me?" the boss demanded.

"No, we're not *trying*," Vinnie answered in a smug tone.

"How much do you have in mind?" the boss hissed after a pause. Dan took a second picture and moved to the next picture.

"One hundred fifty more. For each of us," Ricco said.

Dan pressed the shutter. *Another snapshot for the family album,* he thought.

"A hundred and fifty!" The boss spat out after a hesitation. "Alright, alright. But you'd better not botch this job like the ones at the farm supply or hardware stores, or I'll do some anonymous spilling of my own to the cops."

A train roared by on the tracks outside, smothering the sound from Dan's camera. *Click! Click! Click!* He was starting to become woozy from all the blood rushing to his head.

"Hey! Those ain't our fault!" Ricco protested.

"Never mind, Ricco," Vinnie chuckled, rubbing his hands together eagerly. "We'll make sure this one goes without a hitch."

"That's why I'm here." The boss crossed his arms. "To make sure I get my money's worth. Especially now, since it's costing more."

"Don't worry, boss. You will, you will. With all this paint and stuff, this whole place is going up like a—" As Vinnie made a sweeping gesture with one hand, he looked up, and his eyes met Dan's.

The look of shock on Vinnie's face was exactly like it was at the office. His brow furrowed, his mouth dropped open in disbelief, and he stepped back, pointing a finger at Dan as if to confirm what he was seeing. His expression shifted from surprise to confusion as he shook his head, as though trying to clear it. "It's the same kid who was outside the window!"

"Up! Up! Up!" Dan called to Paul, but he didn't have to say anything. His brother was already dragging Dan over the lip of the shaft.

Paul pulled Dan up, and the boys tumbled to the ground in a tangled heap. They both scrambled to get up and raced towards the staircase, negotiating the labyrinth of shelves and pallets in almost complete darkness. To Dan, each step was one of a million miles, performed in agonizing slowness as fear drove them forward. Just as the pair reached the top of the stairs, Vinnie and Ricco charged into the hallway below. Their flashlights glared in Dan and Paul's faces.

"There they are!" Ricco cried. The light glinted off the barrel of the gun he held in his free hand.

"No shooting in here!" Vinnie ordered. "We've got stuff set up. A stray shot could start the fire while we're still in here!"

"Get 'em!" Ricco's voice bounced off the walls in the tight corridor.

Paul grabbed Dan's arm. "Down the shaft!"

The brothers dashed towards the freight elevator, but it was too late. The rumbling cab had been activated and was already gliding downwards past their floor. It halted below on the first level, sealing off their only hope of escape. There was no way out.

Vinnie and Ricco ran up the staircase, their steps echoing off the walls, their flashlight beams dancing and blazing like fireballs. Dan and Paul split, darting down two different aisles. The hunters stopped at the top of the stairs, then huddled in a heated, whispered conference. Dan stopped partway down one row of shelving and held his breath to listen.

The distant rumble of another train grew, and the floor quivered beneath Dan's feet. The locomotive groaned and wheezed with labored breaths, growing ever louder until it filled every inch with the air. Unlike the faster train that passed earlier, probably a sleek passenger liner, this one must be a slower freight. Its heavy wheels screamed and clacked in a mesmerizing rhythm.

Vinnie and Ricco flicked off their flashlights, shrouding the room in pitch blackness.

The train passed the building slowly. The growling of the engine and the *clack-clack-clack* of the wheels along the tracks stuffed the space with noise. Dan realized it would cover any sound of movement made in the room... allowing the goons to start a dangerous game of cat and mouse, with Dan and Paul as the mice.

Dan's mind raced as he thought about his photos. With every passing second, the crucial experience of working in the darkroom and unloading cameras with no light kicked in. He quickly rewound the film and opened the camera back, retrieving the film canister and slipping it into his pocket before closing the camera. Pressing his back against a rack, he placed the camera among some paint cans, as if he were trying to hide it.

He froze, his every nerve alive with tension. He didn't know but rather sensed someone near him, a tingling sensation in the air that he couldn't explain.

*****

Paul sprinted down one aisle. He collided with a wall and came to a stop, his breath in ragged gasps. At the end of the line of shelves, Vinnie and Ricco stood close together in the dull glow of flashlights, their words soft and indiscernible. Paul strained to make out what they were saying, but couldn't. They extinguished their flashes, casting the area into pitch black.

He stayed put. His hearing was good; he'd be able to pick up if either of them moved toward him. But where was Dan?

Paul felt the vibrations more than heard the thundering of the oncoming train as it drew closer. Louder and louder, the rumbling of the locomotive grew until it swept away all other sounds in its wake. The clack and shrill scream of iron wheels along the rails churned up a dreadful cacophony that even the noise of a marching army would be lost inside it. Paul automatically assumed the boxer's stance. He strained to pick up anything to show if Vinnie or Ricco had moved.

He turned, head cocked, alert. A hand grabbed him on his shoulder and spun him around.

***

Dan's eyes darted around the darkness, searching for any sign of movement. Then he spotted it: an inky shadow slipping swiftly down the shelves toward him. The train passed the building. The night grew silent again, except for the sounds of a struggle from another aisle. The clash of blows, muffled grunts and shifting feet were followed by a groan and a thud, marking the fall of a body. Dan wondered whose.

The noise of the fight distracted Dan long enough that the shadow he had seen—he recognized it as Vinnie—lunged towards him. The two grappled against the shelves, an ugly, chaotic wrestling and clutching match, not anything like the gloriously choreo-graphed fights Dan had seen in the movies. Vinnie clamped one arm around Dan's neck while wrenching the other up behind his back.

"I got one!" Vinnie shouted.

"I've taken care of the other one!" Ricco yelled back.

Vinnie hustled Dan to the end of the aisle. A flashlight shone straight into his eyes.

"What did you do to my brother?" Dan demanded.

The light bounced a little as Ricco chuckled coldly. "I just re-turned a favor. He's back there on the floor, taking a little snooze."

Vinnie looked down at Dan. "Okay, punk, what did you do with the camera?"

"I don't know what—" Dan replied.

Vinnie yanked Dan's arm up. Dan cried out as pain shot through his body like a lightning bolt. "Where's the camera you had? Takin' pictures of us. I saw ya."

"What are talking about? You're seeing things, pal," Dan gasped out through a grimace. He screamed as Vinnie increased the pres-sure. "Okay, okay, you're breaking my arm! Down that aisle. I hid it behind some paint cans."

"Check that out," Vinnie commanded.

Ricco trotted down the aisle. In a moment, he returned holding the camera. Dan hoped the goon was too dumb to see the picture counter showed "zero".

"Thought you were smart, eh, punk?" Ricco sneered, waving his finger at Dan.

"Yes, actually," Dan shot back.

Ricco backhanded Dan across the face. "No wisecracks, see?"

Dan worked his jaw back and forth a couple of times. "Yeah."

"Hey, how did these kids find us?" Ricco asked Vinnie. He jabbed his finger at Dan. "Well, punk, how?"

"I suppose it was just a lucky guess," Dan retorted. That earned him another backhand. The warm iron taste of blood seeped into his mouth.

"Somebody must have told him," Vinnie said, "and it ain't one of us. You can bet the boss didn't."

"Well?" Ricco demanded. When Dan didn't answer, the goon unleashed a flurry of body blows. "How about now? Ready to talk?"

Dan gasped for breath and shook his head.

"Tough guy, huh?" Ricco sneered. He repeated the beating. "Now?"

"I... won't... talk..." Dan groaned out.

"It had to be somebody who knows our plans," Vinnie said.

Ricco jerked his thumb toward one side of the building. "What about the other kid waiting in the car? The one you hired at the YMCA? I never did trust him."

"Jake didn't tell us anything!" Dan blurted out. He regretted doing so at once. *Stupid, stupid, stupid,* he thought.

"What's this? I didn't mention any names, did I, Ricco?" Vinnie gloated.

"No, you didn't," Ricco answered with a grin. "There's the answer to who the stoolie is. He must have let these two in. Thanks, smart guy."

The two goons chortled.

"What are we going to do with them?" Ricco asked. "Take them to lunch?"

Vinnie chuckled. "Nah, not lunch. A barbecue. We'll take care of them all at once. Tie him up."

"With what?" Ricco protested. "I don't carry a bunch of rope in case I have to tie somebody up!"

Vinnie looked around. "There's some packing tape on that carton. Use that."

Ricco grabbed the heavy metal dispenser, tore some tape off, and sealed it on Dan's mouth. "That'll stop your wisecracks." He followed that up by ripping off a longer piece and wounded several loops around Dan's wrists.

"Bring the camera, Ricco." Vinnie shoved Dan toward the stairs. "Get moving, you. Upstairs."

Dan made his way up the steps, stumbling sometimes because of the erratic illumination of the flashlight held by Ricco, his heart pounding in his chest. In his mind, he desperately sought a solution and an escape from this situation. However, every road he explored only pointed towards an unavoidable and fatal outcome. It was like a man condemned to death as he mounted the thirteen steps higher and higher towards the gallows.

The group reached the third floor, a vast space lined with tall shelves filled with cartons and paint cans, just as the second was. At the center of the room, a large, ominous-looking wooden crate lay open like a coffin, its hinged lid to one side. Packing material from inside had been pulled out and lay strewn about. As they drew closer, a sharp scent of turpentine hit Dan's nostrils. He figured the straw-like packing from the box must be soaked with the stuff. Vinnie moved Dan to stand at the end of the box, heels against the wood.

"That will make good kindling." Vinnie pointed to the camera, and Ricco tossed it on the packing material. "Now, wise guy, you want to know what is going to happen? You gonna get the inside story... from inside this crate."

Vinnie gave Dan a shove, and he fell backward, hard, into the box with a groan. Vinnie slammed the lid shut with a cruel finality before locking it with the metal latch, the sound echoing ominously in Dan's ears.

"Now, let's take care of the others. I got something extra special planned for the squealer," Vinnie said, "but we've got to work fast."

The rasp of a match lighting, then the sounds of footsteps rapidly leaving. A few moments later, Dan smelled smoke and heard the menacing crackle of flames from outside the crate.

Chapter Sixteen

The rough wooden boards dug into Dan's back as he fought against the tape binding his wrists, but they held firm, unyielding to his struggles. Flames roared and spat outside the oblong box, the crackling growing louder and the heat intensifying in the confined space. Panic threatened to consume him as he frantically searched for an escape from a living cremation.

With a primal roar, he twisted his body and lunged towards the lid, slamming his shoulder into the top with brute force. The wood buckled slightly under the impact, but the stubborn latch refused to budge. Dan gritted his teeth and tried again and again. He gave up, sore, exhausted and defeated by the unyielding obstacle above him.

Dan searched his prison for another way out. It was made of wooden planks, nailed to a two-by-four frame. *Okay, if I can't break the top open, maybe I can force out the nails holding the ends,* he reasoned.

He shifted his body, drawing up his knees as far as he could. With every ounce of strength he could muster, he slammed his feet against one end, trying to separate the edge from the side.

"Harder, harder, harder." He urged himself on, dedicating each kick to somebody. One for Mom, one for Donna, and especially one for his brother.

The roaring inferno threatened to engulf the crate, sending searing waves of heat inside. Sweat dripped off his face. With each try, Dan could feel the wood giving way, the nails releasing their grip slowly and unwillingly, but time was running out.

Dan continued to kick the end of the box. This one for Betty, this one for Mr. Wilson...

At last, the wood broke away, splintering and peeling away from one corner. He laughed in relief as he attacked the opposite corner until it too jerked free, then he sent the panel dancing away with a final kick. Wriggling like a worm, he slid out of the casket-like space, the tape over his mouth muffling his triumphant shout. He got to his feet.

Flames licked at the edges of the crate. The fire on this floor was growing rapidly, the blaze tickling the roof.

Dan scanned the smoke-filled room, his heart pounding in his chest. He searched for any sign of his brother among the boiling smoke and flames, wondering if Vinnie and Ricco had hauled him upstairs as well. Screaming Paul's name, he desperately listened for an answer, but the tape over his mouth muffled his voice and was also drowned out by the roar of the inferno. He tried again, straining to make himself heard above the chaos, but still, nothing came from his twin.

Finally, a faint answer struggled to be heard through the crackling inferno. It seemed to come from the floor below. Dan stumbled down the smoke-filled staircase.

"Paul, hang on! I'm coming!" Dan shouted through his gag. He knew he wouldn't be understood, but he wanted Paul to know he was on his way.

The intense heat assaulted Dan as he reached the lower floor, his eyes stinging and watering. He blinked several times, trying to clear his vision. The stack of turpentine-soaked palettes blazed. Paul was tied to a rack near the bonfire, like a witch being burned at the stake. The wood piled at Paul's feet was smoldering.

"Paul!" Dan yelled through his gag. "Hold on!"

Paul turned his head towards Dan, his face wet with sweat. His eyes were wide with terror but also filled with relief at seeing his twin.

Dan looked around, spotting the dispenser that Ricco had used to get the tape that bound him. Dan carefully stepped backward towards it and reached out for the hefty metal object with his hands. He awkwardly positioned the dispenser to hold it with the cutting edge facing outward and made his way towards his brother.

The pieces of palettes next to Paul's feet ignited, and Paul moved back as much as possible and stood on his tiptoes. Dan positioned the dispenser's teeth against the tape on Paul's wrists and started to saw. The cutting edge bit into the tape and, with swift, firm motions, until Dan sliced through it.

Paul pulled his hands apart as his bonds separated and fell away. He jumped off the wood, grabbing Dan and pulling him away from the flames. "Thanks, buddy. Your turn," Paul said after rip-ping the gag from his own mouth and tossing it aside. He grabbed the dispenser from Dan and cut through the tape that wrapped around his brother's wrists.

"At last!" Dan tore his own gag off, wincing at the sting it left behind.

"Let's get out of here!" Paul said.

"We can't yet. Vinnie and Ricco said they were gonna 'take care' of Jake. He could be in here, too." Dan's sweeping gesture took in the entire burning warehouse. "Somewhere."

"Are you serious?" Paul asked as he dropped the dispenser on the floor.

"That's what they said," Dan answered. "They worked me over and I let his name slip."

"Then we've gotta find him before it's too late!" Paul said.

"Jake! JAKE!" Dan shouted.

Paul's voice rang out, "Jake!" Tears streamed down his face as he struggled to see through the growing smoke and again he yelled out Jake's name. The brothers stood still, straining to hear a response amidst the chaos of the fire. "Come on, Jake, give us some idea of where you are," Paul pleaded under his breath.

"Jake! Please, man, if you're in here, let us know where you are!" Dan's desperation grew with each passing second, his eyes smarting from the smoke as he coughed. The heat radiating from the flames that consumed the burning palettes threatened to bake them like a roast in the oven.

"Jake!" Paul called out again.

"Jake!" Dan shouted. "Please, just make some kind of sound! Anything!"

Suddenly, a faint but unmistakable response reached them.

"Did you catch that?" Dan asked, grabbing Paul's arm.

"Sounds like he's downstairs!" Paul confirmed, and without hesitation, they both rushed toward the stairwell, nearly tripping over debris and dodging falling embers.

The two stumbled down the stairs, lit by the flickering light of the flames. The first floor was ablaze, with three different fires burning. It looked like Vinnie and Ricco were living up to their pledge to the boss to make this job "perfect".

"Damn it! Look what they've done!" Dan cursed under his breath and pointed.

Gagged, suspended by his wrists over one of the raging fires, Jake dangled helplessly. The rope holding him was looped over a pipe and tied off by the door.

"We're coming, Jake!" Paul looked at Dan for guidance. "What do we do?"

Dan mumbled, "I don't know."

The two stood for a minute, helpless.

"Untying him would drop him into the flames," Dan thought aloud, squinting through the smoke. "We need to pull him up and away. Or back and away. Any direction but down."

"Hey, I've got an idea. Untie that rope, but hold on tight." Paul pushed his brother toward it.

"Why? What are you going to do?" Dan asked.

"I've never played football, but now it's time to learn how to tackle." Paul gripped the cord and tugged, taking the tension off the knot. "Loosen it now!"

Dan undid the knot and hung onto the rope. "Got it."

"I'll tell you know when to let go," Paul said. "Are you ready?"

"Ready as I'll ever be!" Dan shouted back, his knuckles turning white from gripping the rope.

"Okay, here goes nothing," Paul muttered.

Paul backed up a few steps and blew out his breath a couple of times. He charged forward with as much speed as he could. Just before reaching the flames, launched himself at Jake in a flying tackle. Wrapping his arms around Jake's waist, he yelled to Dan, "Now!"

Dan released the rope. At the same time, Paul threw his legs in front of him. He and Jake somersaulted forward and then to the floor in a tangle of limbs, narrowly avoiding the flames that burned below them. Getting up, Paul hustled Jake around one side of the fire.

"Thanks," Jake coughed out as they reached Dan. "I owe you one."

"Anytime, buddy," Paul grinned. He set to work untying Jake, wincing as he saw the deep red marks left by the tight bonds. "Are you okay?"

"Yeah." Jake rubbed his wrists.

Explosions shook the room as paint thinner containers burst, dumping more fuel into the inferno. The flaming liquid flooded the floor.

"Guys, we need to get out. Like, now," Dan said. "This place is going up fast."

"You bet." Paul jerked his thumb over his shoulder. "Back to the door we came in."

The crackling sound of the flames chased them down the hallway to the exterior door. Dan tried the knob. He swore. "They locked it... or jammed it, or something, but it won't open!" He felt around. "It's keyed on both sides."

Jake coughed as smoke filled the corridor. "We can't breathe this stuff much longer."

Dan stripped to the waist and held out his hand. "Quick! Give me your shirts."

Paul and Jake took off their shirts, tossing them to Dan. He bolted into the cramped bathroom, flipped on the light, and soaked the garments in the sink until they were drenched with water. He threw them back to the others.

"Tie your it around your mouth and nose, like a mask," Dan said as he did so. "The cloth will filter the smoke. Well, some of it."

Dan and Jake tied their wet shirts around their mouths and noses.

"Now what?" Jake asked.

"Find a way out! The loading dock doors!" Paul ran back to the main room, followed by the others. "There they are!"

The trio dashed over the debris-strewn floor, their arms shielding their faces from the heat that felt like it was peeling off their skin. Flames flicked hungrily at the walls, casting eerie shadows that danced and squirmed like living things. Cans of paint thinner burst open, vomiting more flaming liquid onto the concrete.

Paul angrily yanked at the padlocks securing the metal roll-up doors and looked around. The fire blocked the exit that probably led to the front office. "Let's head for the roof!"

Retracing their steps, they raced back to the hallway and started upstairs. With a roaring crash, a shelf on the second floor collapsed, spilling flaming liquid over the head of the stairs.

"The power is still on," Dan pointed to the light in the bathroom. "What about—"

"The elevator!" Paul finished. "Come on!"

Sweat dripped down their bodies and faces, stinging their eyes. The group rushed for the freight elevator. They piled in.

Dan hit the button, and the elevator jolted into motion. His attention shifted to the slow, rumbling ascent of the cab. "These things aren't built for speed."

The elevator made it halfway between the first and second floors, grumbled, then shuddered. It stopped.

"Damn it! The fire's reached the fusebox! The power's off!" Jake cursed, slamming his fist against the wall. "Now what?"

"Up there!" Dan pointed. The cab had no door, and the top half was open to the second floor. "We can climb out through that gap."

"Give me a boost." Jake slapped Paul on the shoulder.

Paul took a deep breath and hoisted Jake up. With a grunt, Jake pulled himself through the space between the second floor and the roof of the cab.

"Come on, guys, hurry," Jake held out his hand. "Move it."

With Dan gripping Jake's hand tightly, Paul lifted with all his strength while Jake pulled from the top, dragging Dan out and onto the floor. Working together, Jake and Dan pulled Paul up as well.

"We've got to keep going," Dan said as some more crates burst into flames.

They sprinted through the smoke, their lungs burning and their vision obscured. The three staggered, more than climbed, the stairs to the top floor.

"Almost there," Paul gasped, reaching the top of the stairs. "The roof access is just ahead."

"Keep going!" Dan shouted over the roar of the fire.

They reached the door to the roof and crowded into it. Dan twisted the knob.

"Locked!" he said.

"Unbolt it, you idiot!" Paul pointed to the deadbolt thumb lever.

"Oh." Dan unlocked the door.

As they burst onto the roof, the fresh air hit them like a refreshing wave. They pulled their shirts away from their noses and slipped them back on, shivering at their clamminess. In the distance, sirens approached.

"What do we do now?" Jake asked. "Just wait for the firemen and their net?"

"We can't stay here," Dan said as he looked around. "The roof may cave in."

Jake pointed to the neighboring warehouse. "If we can get to that other building, we'd be safer."

"Are you crazy?" Paul said. "There is no way to jump over there! It's too far!"

Dan scanned the roof and spotted a weathered wooden extension ladder lying near one corner. He waved at it. "We can't jump it, but here's something I think can help."

"That won't reach the ground, genius," Paul snarled.

Looking between the ladder and the structure next door, Dan estimated the ladder's length and the distance to the other building. "It won't reach down, my dear brother, but it may reach across."

"You're nuts!" Paul exploded.

"That is quite possible, but I don't want to be a roasted one," Dan said. "Shut up and give me a hand."

The three hauled the ladder to the edge of the roof and pulled it out until it was almost fully extended. With some effort, they placed it in a way that connected the gap between the two buildings. It was a tight fit, but it just barely reached across.

"Dan, are you sure this will work?" Paul asked.

"Absolutely positive. Ninety-nine percent," Dan said, his voice steady despite the fear gnawing at his insides. "We don't have any other choice."

"I'll cross first, and steady it at the other end," Jake offered.

"Okay," Paul said. "Just... be careful, alright?"

"Always am when I'm not in the ring," Jake flashed a quick smile before crawling on the makeshift bridge. "Here goes nothing."

Dan and Paul held their breath, watching Jake inch his way across the space between the buildings, his hands shaking from the effort. The wooden ladder flexed dangerously under his weight, creaking and groaning with each movement. Hours seemed to pass as Jake crawled to the other side. At last, he climbed onto the roof of the neighboring warehouse.

"Made it!" He waved his arms for emphasis. He leaned on the end of the ladder, securing it. "All right! Got it! It's stable!"

"Great Jake!" Dan called out, relief washing over him. "Paul, you're up!"

Paul stared at the ladder, then back at his brother, his face pale. He took a step back. "I... I can't."

"What do you mean, you can't? Why not?" Dan said in exasperation.

"Because I'm afraid of heights!" Paul blurted out.

"What!" Dan cried. "I've known you for seventeen years, and now you tell me this?"

"I've never had to climb across a shaky ladder five stories above the ground before, either!" Paul fired back.

"Come on, buddy, we don't have time for this!" Dan said. "You have to cross now or we'll be trapped here!"

"Get moving!" Jake yelled. "The fire trucks are getting closer, but they won't be here in time! Flames are coming out of the roof door!"

"Look, Paul," Dan said, trying to sound as reassuring as possible. "You saw Jake make it safe, right? Just focus on Jake and take it one rung at a time. You'll be okay. I believe in you."

"Can't you just... go without me?" Paul asked weakly. "I'll wait here..."

"We're not breaking up the act," David shot back. "Discussion ended."

Paul shook his head. "I can't."

"You can't stay here! Here, let me put it this way." Dan leaned toward his brother and bellowed. "You're going across that damn ladder if it's the last thing you do!"

Fear in Paul momentarily shifted to anger. "It just maybe, Tarzan!"

Dan gripped Paul's shoulders and spoke through clenched teeth. "Get your rear end across that ladder, or I'll forget I'm your sensitive artist-type twin brother and slug you right in the kisser!" He spun Paul around, shoved him to the ladder, then slapped him on his rump. "Get along, little dogie."

"I hate you," Paul snarled. "Mom should have given you back to the stork when she had the chance."

"She lost the receipt. Now move."

Paul hesitated for a moment before taking a deep, shaky breath and nodding. "Okay."

"Good for you," Dan kept his voice firm but gentle. "Now move forward. Don't look down. You can do it. I know you can."

"Fine, right, bully for me. Rah, rah." Paul crawled onto the ladder. Each rung gave an ominous creak under his weight, but he crept ahead, his breathing labored.

Dan watched his brother's progress, every wobble of the ladder sending a jolt of fear through him. Paul froze midway across, staring down at the ground below.

"Don't look down! I told you! Don't look down! Keep your eyes on Jake! Concentrate on Jake! Keep going, buddy!" Dan urged.

"Come on, Paul, keep moving!" Jake shouted. "I don't want to train another sparring partner!"

Paul didn't move. He shook his head.

"Okay, I'm coming behind you." Dan moved onto the ladder. It creaked and complained, sagging under the added weight. Dan reached Paul. "I'm in back of you. We fall, we fall together. You don't want that, I'm sure. I know I don't. Keep going. For me... for us. One for all and all for whatever it is."

Paul swallowed hard and resumed his slow crawl forward, one shaky rung at a time, Dan following close behind, encouraging his brother. The two crossed as if picking their way through a minefield.

"You're almost there, Paul!" Dan said.

The ladder wobbled and protested. With a final surge, Paul reached the other side. Heaving himself onto the roof, he let out an audible sigh. "I made it!"

"I knew you could, buddy!" Dan called out. "Make room! Here I come!"

A snap came from under Dan, the sound of wood splitting. The ladder tilted to one side. Dan hurried forward, one foot slipping through the rungs. He pulled his leg up and continued toward the other roof, the ladder vibrating up and down like the string of a

musical instrument. He nearly reached the other side when the
ladder split in two.

Chapter Seventeen

Dan's heart tried to climb out of his mouth as he swung down, hurtling towards the ground. He instinctively squeezed his eyes shut and braced for his smashing on the asphalt, but instead came the jarring thud of the ladder slamming against the brick wall. His eyes snapped open as he dangled, his fingers gripping tightly to the rungs. He looked up at Paul and Jake, hanging onto the top rung, their faces contorted with sheer determination and their muscles tense as they fought to save Dan from the deadly fall.

"Here, boy! Come! Come!" Paul grunted through clenched teeth. "We can't wait forever!"

Dan began to pull himself up, one agonizing rung at a time.

"Almost there, Dan!" Paul groaned out. "Keep coming, buddy!"

With one last effort, Dan gripped the edge of the roof and pulled himself up with a grunt. Paul and Jake let go of the ladder, helping Dan as crawled onto the surface. The ladder made a loud, splintering crash on the pavement below, causing them all to wince.

"Let's not do that again anytime soon." Paul's chest heaved as he tried to catch his breath.

"You said it." Dan gave a weak grin. "I can see it now in the yearbook, next to my picture: 'Voted Most Likely to Hang off the Side of a Building Twice in One Week.'"

Paul helped Dan to his feet. "Hey, how about drawing a comic book with a crime-fighting hero who can climb up walls by himself?"

Dan brushed off his pants. "Nah, nobody would buy that."

"Cut the chatter and let's get down from here." Jake pointed to a fire escape on the far side of the roof. The three boys hurried toward it, the sound of approaching sirens blaring. Jake went down first. Dan stopped Paul.

"Will you be okay climbing down?" Dan asked, concerned. "It's pretty high."

Paul grinned and gave a thumbs-up. "Just watch me, my dear brother, just watch me! Piece of cake!"

They reached the ground as the flames roared and broke through the paint building's roof with a roar. The fire trucks screeched to a stop in front. Firefighters in full gear jumped out, pulling out hoses and axes from their trucks and quickly springing into action.

"Hey! You guys! How did you get here?" A voice boomed out.

Dan turned to Paul. "He sounds familiar."

Paul nodded. "Why, I believe it is our old friend…"

"Where did you kids come from?" Detective Barton stalked over to the trio, accompanied by the crunch of gravel under heavy footsteps. He planted his fists on his hips and glared at them.

"Well, just a few minutes ago, we came from there." Dan jerked his thumb toward the brick warehouse. "But before that, we came from over there." He pointed burning paint company. He snapped his fingers and spoke to his brother. "We left our jackets inside."

"What!" Barton's face turned as red as the flames, veins pulsing in his neck and forehead. "Didn't I tell you boys to stay out of this? Didn't I tell you to leave the crime-solving to the professionals?"

"Do you really want an answer?" Paul asked with an innocent smile.

"No! I have a good mind to run you in! For trespassing, for interfering with a criminal investigation…" Barton stopped and pointed to what Dan had pulled from his pocket and held up in his hand. "What's that thing?"

"Just some exposed film." Dan turned the small canister slightly. "Is there a darkroom at the police station?"

The detective raised an eyebrow. "Yes. Why?"

"Because," Dan lifted the film a little higher in triumph, "this little baby contains pictures of the crime in progress."

"You… wait… what?" The skepticism and confusion in Barton's voice were unmistakable.

"He was hanging upside down at the time when he took them. In there." Paul pointed to the paint company building. "I was holding him by his ankles down an elevator shaft."

"I have photos of the arsonists at work, and the big boss as well." Dan could almost feel the detective's doubt floating heavily in the air between them. "Trust me, Detective, you'll want to see these."

"Alright, kid." Barton sighed. "We've got a darkroom at the station. We'll see what you've got. Let's get going."

As they followed Barton towards the waiting police cars, Paul nudged Dan and said in a low voice, "Remember, we each get one phone call."

***

Paul fidgeted in the brightly lit office of Detective Barton, his fingers drumming nervously on the cold metal armrest of the chair. Dan had disappeared into the darkroom to develop his photos, leaving Paul alone to give his statement in a small, suffocating, windowless room. Now it was Jake's turn to be questioned. After what felt like years, Barton finally entered and sat down at his desk, slipping a few sheets of paper into a thick file.

"Where's Jake?" Paul couldn't help but ask.

"He's in a holding cell," the detective answered.

"A holding cell!" Paul jumped to his feet. "Why?"

"He's an accessory to the crime."

Paul leaned on the desk. "He was only the lookout! He had nothing to do with the crimes!"

"That's still being an accessory."

"But he told us what was going on!" Paul protested.

The detective jabbed his index finger at Paul. "Which you should have relayed to me."

Paul threw up his hands and shouted. "Okay, okay, we should have called. In that case, put Dan and me in that holding cell, too!" He held his wrists out for the handcuffs.

Barton waved Paul back down in his chair. "Simmer down now Paul, just simmer down."

Paul sat, then paused a second to cool down. "Look, I think Jake's a good guy down deep. He just made a stupid decision."

"I tend to agree with you, but it's out of my hands," Barton said. "It's his first offense, and he's young. He'll probably get probation. Maybe even less, if he becomes a witness for the state."

"Sorry for yelling," Paul said.

"That's okay." Barton regarded Paul. "Jake said he met you when you two sparred at the YMCA."

"Yeah."

"Perhaps I'll swing by one night and join you two."

"You box?"

"When I was in the Navy. During the war, it helped break up the shipboard monotony between the sheer terror of battles." Barton grinned ruefully. "I haven't been in the ring for years. I'm probably out of shape and out of practice."

Paul returned the grin. "Come to the YMCA. Jake and I will give you a workout."

Dan bustled into the room. He carried a rod, with four photos clipped onto it. "Don't touch them, they're still wet." He held the pictures in front of the detective and explained with pride, "I extended the development time to increase the effective film speed and improve the exposure. The contrast and grain are up, but you definitely can make out the faces."

"Who am I looking at here?" Barton leaned forward to examine the images.

Paul got up and moved around to peek over his shoulder. "Those two big lugs, they are the arsonists." He pointed. "He's Ricco Toccini, and the other one's first name is Vinnie."

"There's one missing. He worked as the frontman, the guy selling the 'insurance'," Dan said. "He goes by Mac Slater of the North Brandale Insurance Company, but he probably changes aliases as often as he does his underwear."

"How did you find out their names?" The detective was astonished.

"We just nosed around a bit. The short, pudgy one is the boss," Dan indicated the man in the picture. "We don't know his name. Oh, yeah, they're renting an office in the same building as La Dolce Vita restaurant, under the name 'Murdstone, Inc.'. It's empty of anything but furniture. They use it for meetings."

The detective looked at the two with amazement. "How on earth did you..." He held up one hand. "Never mind. Don't tell me. I don't want to know."

He returned to staring at the photos for a minute. Opening the top drawer of his desk, he fumbled through the contents, then removed a magnifying glass, examining one particular photo through it.

Dan looked at Paul and pointed. "Hey, detectives really use those things."

"Shut up," Barton growled. Paul put an index finger to his lips and shushed his brother.

After a careful inspection of the photo, the detective leaned back in his chair and tapped the magnifying glass against his cheek, lost in thought. Suddenly, he spun around and began rummaging through a small bookcase behind him. He pulled out an old program for the 1946 Policemen versus Firemen Charity Football Game and quickly flipped through the pages. Finding what he was looking for, he slapped the open booklet on his desk and used his index finger to circle an advertisement. He looked up at Dan. "Is this the same man? The one you said was the boss?"

Dan read the ad. "Melvin Johnson, Bookkeeper and Tax Accountant." He nodded. "Yep. The guy in the ad is the same one I took the photo of tonight."

Paul arched one eyebrow. "An accountant running a protection racket?"

"Perhaps he wanted more money than his practice was providing and wanted to expand." Dan thought about it for a moment. "I'm willing to bet that the common thread among all the victims is that they are, or were, clients of this Melvin Johnson person. It makes sense. That's how he selected who to sell his protection to. Being their accountant, he would know all about their financial situations. Based on that, he figured out who to target and how much they could afford to pay in tributes."

Barton nodded. "That's solid reasoning."

"It comes from all the cheap detective magazines he reads," Paul put in.

"He'll finish *Fun with Dick and Jane* any year now," Dan returned.

Barton chuckled as he stood. Taking the photos, he headed for the door. "I'll get a dragnet thrown out for these guys immediately. Jake provided a description of the car." He stopped in the doorway and turned around. "By the way, your mother should be here very soon."

"You called Mom!" the brothers cried out at once.

"Yes. It's department policy. You both are underage, so your parent has to be notified." The detective left the room.

Dan faced his brother. "We're dead."

"I hope he warned the desk sergeant," Paul said. He clutched Dan's arm. "Too late! There she is!"

Mrs. Case's voice, speaking in her firm, no-nonsense way she used when she was about to bulldoze through any opposition, sounded at the end of the hall, followed by her crisp, clipped footsteps. Before she reached the office, Barton introduced himself. They appeared at the door.

"I'll have you know, Mrs. Case, your boys did something incredibly dumb tonight," the detective said. "However, it was both courageous and helpful. You should be proud of them."

Their mother's eyes roamed over her two sons. They both had washed their hands and faces, removing the soot. However, their torn and messy clothing still bore evidence of being in the fire. She crossed her arms and gave them her stern, "now what" look, the one she always wore whenever they got into mischief.

"Well? Who is going to tell me what you two got up to this time?" she asked.

The twins pointed to each other. "He will!" they answered together.

***

Dan squinted through the viewfinder of his new camera, adjusting the aperture and shutter speed to capture the perfect shot of the cheerleaders in their bright red uniforms on the freshly cut green football field. He couldn't wait to see how the photos turned out.

"None of you had to testify in court?" Betty asked Paul.

"Nope," he answered. "The district attorney laid everything out for the protection gang's lawyers. He let them know he had three eyewitnesses—Dan, Jake and I—plus the testimony of all the victims. Not to mention the pictures Dan took of them caught in the act. The DA said the phots were the best witnesses to have. They're silent, and don't get tripped up in cross-examination!"

Dan fiddled with the camera controls yet again. "Vinnie, Ricco, Melvin, and Mac practically fell over each other, snitching on the other ones. They all finally copped a plea."

"What about Jake? I'd like to meet him." Donna linked arms with Dan. "Now don't get jealous, handsome."

Dan's cheeks flushed, and he stammered slightly. "Ah... he's got... Detective Barton was right. Jake was given some probation."

"He'll be joining us at the 'Mr. Wilson's Thank You and Apology Dinner' at the Country Club tomorrow night. So are all the other business people involved," Betty said. She turned to Paul. "I'm glad you and my father talked. Patched things up."

"So am I," Paul said with a grin. "I don't want to run foul of your dad again."

"Come on, everybody. We've got to replace the picture that was on the stolen negatives. We need to hurry," Dan said as he glanced at the sky. "It's the golden hour. I mean, look—"

"At the light!" Paul, Betty and Donna chorused.

Dan grinned, then passed the camera to Paul as though handing over a newborn infant. "Don't touch those dials! They're set correctly…" Betty and Donna grabbed Dan by the arms and pulled him away. "Make sure you can see everybody through the viewfinder!"

Giggling, the girls forced Dan into the oversized bear costume. He struggled to fit his legs through the furry pants before finally slipping them on.

"And don't cut off people's heads!" Dan added.

"Speaking of heads, don't forget yours, handsome." Donna held up the bear's head.

"I don't understand why I must be in this thing," Dan grumbled.

"Remember, my dear brother? I said the next time I'm making you wear that rug while I take the pretty pictures," Paul said.

"Oh, shut up." Dan jammed on the bear's head.

"Alright, girls, get in tight! You're looking great! Cozy up to the bear!" Paul waved the cheerleaders to their positions. "Hey, which button do I push again?"

Dan's muffled voice came out of the costume. "The round one, you dope!"

"Oh, yeah. Okay, here goes!" The camera shutter clicked. "Got it! Do you think I should take a few more, you know, just to be safe?"

"Oh yes, you should," Donna said. "After all, it's called the golden *hour*."

"Yes, of course!" Betty chimed in. "We can take pictures for the next forty-five minutes!"

The bear growled and reached toward Paul with its paws.

"Perfect! That's perfect! Don't move!" Paul snapped off some more shots.

www.ingramcontent.com/pod-product-compliance
Lightning Source LLC
Chambersburg PA
CBHW011921050726
47591CB00007B/2282

9 781962 056021